A BULLET FOR BEN McCABE

Gunned down and left for dead, Ben McCabe is nursed back to health, only to learn that he's wanted for murder and robbery. With no memory of his past, he sets out in search of the truth, gradually putting together the events that led to his shooting. As his memory returns, he tracks down the real killers — but his problems are not over. Lurking in the shadows is a man with the bullet he has saved for Ben McCabe . . .

PETER WILSON

A BULLET FOR BEN MCCABE

Complete and Unabridged

LINFORD
Leicester

First published in Great Britain in 2010 by
Robert Hale Limited
London

First Linford Edition
published 2011
by arrangement with
Robert Hale Limited
London

The moral right of the author has been asserted

British Library CIP Data

Wilson, Peter.
 A bullet for Ben McCabe.- -
 (Linford western library)
 1. Western stories.
 2. Large type books.
 I. Title II. Series
 823.9'2–dc22

 ISBN 978–1–4448–0684–7

Published by
F. A. Thorpe (Publishing)
Anstey, Leicestershire

Set by Words & Graphics Ltd.
Anstey, Leicestershire
Printed and bound in Great Britain by
T. J. International Ltd., Padstow, Cornwall

This book is printed on acid-free paper

1

The brothers found the man late in the morning. He was lying face down, the gently flowing stream lapping against his legs, his head twisted at a strange angle. He was not moving.

Tommy, two years older than his brother, put his fishing rod aside and crept carefully, silently towards the figure in the blood-red shirt.

'Is he dead?' Josh whispered, keeping a safe distance behind.

'Dunno. Looks like.'

'What we gonna do?' asked Josh still whispering, as though fearful that if he spoke too loudly the stricken man would rise up.

'Dunno,' said Tommy again. 'Mebbe we'd better get Grandpa. He'll know what to do.'

Tommy took another look down at man. He still hadn't moved.

'C'mon, Tommy — let's go.' Josh was frightened. He had never seen a dead man before.

The two brothers crept away from the scene and were well out of earshot before they burst into a run, towards the other side of the glade where they had left their grandfather enjoying the sun. He was dozing in the wagon when they rushed up to report their find . . .

★ ★ ★

He heard the voices first . . . far off . . . coming only in urgent gasps. 'He's moving, Ma, he's moving.'

Then a woman whispered, 'Ssh, Josh — go get your grandpa.'

He moved and tried to open his eyes but there was only a blur. His chest ached. And his head. Consciousness was coming slowly and painfully. He was aware of a tightness in his chest as though . . . he was strapped down. He tried to move but the slightest effort brought more pain.

There were more voices, indistinct at first then coming more clearly. Older this time. And closer.

He opened his eyes but everything was a haze. His head fell back on to a soft pillow and he gasped for air.

The older voice came again. 'Don't worry, Beth, our friend's going nowhere.'

The man on the bed opened his eyes fully; this time the view was clear as day. And he was staring down the barrel of a shotgun.

It was the old man who spoke. 'This mayn't kill you, mister, but it will sure make one helluva mess of them good looks.'

The face behind the shotgun came slowly into focus. It was sun baked, creased with age to match the voice. The eyes, pale and blue, were staring coldly into his. A gnarled finger was poised around the trigger. The man closed his eyes, trying to shut out all around him. Where was he? Who were these people? And why was he strapped to a bed?

'He's gone again, Pop.' This time it was a woman's voice and she sounded as though she cared. 'Maybe we ought to leave him some more.'

He felt the man with the shotgun ease himself off the bed and grunt a reluctant agreement.

Then he heard his own voice — it was nothing more than a croak.

'Please . . . whoever you are, don't go . . .'

Again the shotgun was pointed into his face. The tightness in his chest, the ache in his head, the feeling of being tied down . . . what was happening?

Suddenly, from behind the old man, the woman came forward and rested her hand on his brow. It was soft and soothing but it didn't last — the old man pulled her roughly away and moved even closer.

'There's a few questions that need answering before I go for the law.' There was anger in the voice and he stared at the man on the bed looking for some reaction. None came.

'Right, mister,' he said sharply, putting the gun aside. 'Let's start with this.' He reached in his shirt pocket and pulled out a sheet of paper which he shook open and held in front of the wounded man. 'You gonna say this ain't you?'

The man in the bed stared at the paper. It was a wanted poster, carrying the picture of a rugged but clean-shaven man in his thirties. Above the face were the words: WANTED — DEAD OR ALIVE. FOR ROBBERY AND MURDER. And below it in bold type it read: $2000 REWARD. OUTLAW BEN McCABE.

The man stared at it, trying to focus, but the paper was snatched away from him before he had chance to study it closely.

'Pop, let the man rest.' More sympathy from the woman.

'Rest? He ain't gonna rest till he's in Hell, Beth. You've done more than enough for this killer.' Then he turned away and shouted to the boy in the corner. 'Here, Josh! Bring me that mirror. Let this critter take a good look at hisself before we turn him in to the law and get our reward.'

Thrusting the small looking-glass into the stranger's hand, he said, 'Take a good look. Mebbe it ain't as pretty as your picture right now. But it sure as hell is you. You're Ben McCabe and you're wanted for murder.'

The man looked into the mirror. He was wearing several days' growth of untidy greying beard, and his head was wrapped in a bloodstained dressing. The dark eyes looked lifeless.

Suddenly the mirror was snatched from his grasp to be replaced by the Wanted poster.

'That's you, mister. You ain't gonna deny it.'

He slumped back on to the pillow, his mind in a whirl. Maybe the old-timer was right; maybe he was Ben McCabe, a killer on the run. He didn't know for sure — he had just looked into the face of a stranger staring back at him from a hand held mirror.

2

They had told him his name was Ben McCabe — the Wanted poster seemed to confirm it — but was it the truth? And why couldn't he remember? Why did he not recognize the face in the mirror?

Ben McCabe . . . he repeated it over and over again in his mind but still it meant nothing to him.

He studied the strapping across his aching chest and then, for the first time, the ropes around his left wrist tying him to the bedpost. He tried to turn on to his side but the effort proved too much. He felt the sweat oozing from his bandaged forehead.

It was then that she came into the room and this time she was alone. A tall, striking figure with strong features, attractive without being over pretty, she walked over to the bedside table where she rested a bowl. She examined the man on the bed and then nodded towards the strappings that bound him to the bed.

'Sorry about those,' she said quietly. He couldn't place her accent but guessed it was European maybe, or from back East.

But why would he know that?

'It was Pop's idea, but you were running a heavy fever and were thrashing around wildly, as though you were raving. Delirious almost. We had to tie you to keep you down while we . . . ' Her voice tailed off.

'I-I don't remember,' he stammered feebly. 'Tell me what happened, Mrs — '

'Kane — Elspeth Kane, though most people call me Beth.' She reached out and opened the top drawer of a bedside cabinet. She withdrew a bullet which she placed in his hand.

'We had to get that out of your chest. We thought you weren't going to make it.'

'How did I get here?'

She smiled. 'You can thank my two sons for that. They were out fishing at the creek and they saw you lying there. Tommy, he's the oldest, thought maybe you were dead but . . . well, here you are.'

'Still breathing,' he said. There was an uneasy silence before he asked, 'So — why didn't you call for the sheriff? The Wanted poster — two thousand dollars is a lot of money.'

She smiled again, this time it reached her eyes. Pale blue.

'The nearest town's some half-a-day's ride away and, the state you were in, we weren't in any serious danger from anything you might do.'

'And it was you who patched me up? No doctor?'

'Me and Pop both. He was a kind of doctor years back. And we had to get the bullet out of you. The one that got you in the head, well it seems that just went bouncing by after it had clipped your temple. You were lucky.'

'Thanks,' he said.

'I've — er — I've brought you some broth. You should try to eat.'

It was his turn to smile. 'How?' He wriggled his left wrist to remind her that he was still tied down.

She hesitated before walking round the bed to untie his hand. Once there, she hesitated again.

'You're not sure about me, are you?' he prompted.

'Pop thinks I should have turned you in days ago, as soon as he saw that poster when he was in town and I — '

'Days! How long have I been here like this?'

'Almost a week,' she answered.

'You've nursed me for a week, and' — he stumbled on — 'why?'

She shrugged. 'Because . . . well you needed help and even if you are what that bill says, like I said, you were hardly in a fit state to take us all.'

She leaned down and started to untie the ropes on his wrist.

'Maybe I'm taking a chance now except I think even I could win a race with you for that gunbelt on the wall over there.'

He looked to where she was pointing. His belt, complete with his Colt was hanging behind the bedroom door.

As she worked at the ropes she asked him, 'Is it true you can't remember who you are? Or — '

He interrupted before she could finish the challenge. 'It's true, Mrs Kane — Beth — I can't remember anything. I just hope that if I am this Ben McCabe that there's been some mistake and that I'm not a thief and a killer.'

'I hope so, too,' she said and left the room.

★   ★   ★

The man who had settled for the name Ben McCabe spent the next two days confined to his bed at the Kane farmhouse during which time he learned as much as he could about the family who had collectively saved his life. Only Pop seemed to be unsure that they had done the right thing. And McCabe learned that the woman's description of him as a 'kind of doctor years back' referred to his days as a veterinary. A horse doctor.

Beth was the widow of Erskine Kane, a former US marshal turned farmer. When he retired as a lawman, the family — Kane, his wife and sons Tommy and Josh — moved out of town and set up their small farm. For three years the family thrived, supplying local traders with corn and other produce.

But Marshal Kane had left behind some bitter and vengeful victims of his honest brand of law enforcement, and some of them did not want to forget.

It was one of those who gunned him down in the heat of a summer's evening as he left the general store after a delivery to one of his regular customers. The killer was a small-time thief whom Kane had thrown in jail on more than one occasion. He had spent the day in the saloon and had spotted the former lawman purely by chance. Without warning he had drawn his gun and fired. The bullet hit the target full in the square of the back, a pointless killing of a well-liked family man.

Left alone to raise two growing boys, Beth had contemplated selling up and returning to schoolteaching but when her husband's father stepped in with an offer of help she agreed to carry on at the farm. Slowly she came to terms with the loss of the man in her life and as the boys grew stronger so the farm, with Pop's guidance, continued to prosper.

Beth and the two boys spent a lot of time around McCabe's bed trying to help him regain his lost memory and all three said things that made him feel that they wanted to believe in him.

Only Pop — Walter Kane — remained unconvinced, even hostile, towards the man he still regarded as an outlaw . . . maybe still a dangerous one. As far as he was concerned the man in the back room was a killer with a $2,000 price on his head.

Why had he allowed Beth to persuade him to save the man's life when it would have been far easier to let him die and collect the reward? No obligations — no complications. Instead, he was recovering in the comfort of their home.

McCabe — for that was how he had come to identify himself — was well aware of the old man's antagonism but he comforted himself with the feeling that the boys and, to a lesser degree their mother, were actually developing a fondess for the stranger they had dragged back from the brink of death. Little did he realize that he would soon have to rely on their growing relationship — and even the older man — as his past came to plague them all.

*　*　*

As the days passed, McCabe regained his physical strength but his mind, as far as his past was concerned, remained a blank. Almost daily, he took out the wanted poster and gazed into the face of the man with a $2,000 reward on his head. Clean shaven and hair trimmed, he was forced to concede that he was that man.

But who had he robbed and who had he killed? And where did it happen? Nothing would come.

Slowly, as his strength returned, McCabe set out to repay the family for all that they had done to help him on the road to recovery.

He joined the old man in the fields, ploughing, digging, chopping wood and helping to repair some of the outbuildings damaged in the winter snows.

It was the night of young Tommy's thirteenth birthday, in the third week after he had been dragged from the creek, that McCabe knew the time had come to think about his future.

Beth had baked one of her special cakes to follow the family meal and the boys were in their beds when McCabe said his good night and retired to his room at the back of the house, leaving

Pop and his son's widow to enjoy the remains of the day.

He dropped off to sleep almost immediately, but whether it was the sound of muffled voices, or the wind that was getting up, he was soon awake and staring up at the ceiling.

The voices came in whispers but there was an urgency about them that caught his attention.

'We're gonna have to tell him, Beth,' Pop was saying, 'the boys are getting fond of him and — '

'And what, Pop?'

'Listen, Beth, don't take this the wrong way, but, well, we don't know enough about him. He could be the killer the poster says.'

Beth tried to keep her voice low. 'Does he act like a killer to you? Far as I can tell he's just a man who got shot up and can't remember.'

'Can't he? Who says so? Look, Beth, maybe this is none of my business but are . . . are you taking to this man?'

There was no immediate reply and

16

the old man hurried on, 'I've seen the way he looks at you and to be honest, it ain't the way a man should be lookin' at a widow woman with two growing boys.'

Beth let out a stifled giggle.

'And how should that be, Pop? If Ben is interested in me he sure hasn't let me know. And what if he was — would that be so bad?'

'You know it would, Beth. D'you want your boys — Erskine's boys — brought up around a man who's more 'n likely a killer?'

'We don't know he's a killer,' Beth protested, but the old man was having none of it.

'An' we don't know he ain't. Look, Beth, I think it best if I tell him to leave. I know the boys'll be upset at first but they'll get over it.'

This time there was no protest. Taking that as her agreement, he added, 'I'll do it when I get back from town tomorrow night.'

In the bedroom McCabe, who had

strained to listen to the conversation, flopped back and stared again at the ceiling.

Some of what the old man had said was true. He had taken to looking on Beth Kane as more than somebody who had offered help and comfort to a stranger in distress. She was a good-looking woman still in her prime and widowhood did not suit her. She was also a good mother to the two boys who, in turn, idolized her. But — and it was the 'but' that old Walter had raised — would he eventually bring trouble to the family?

He fell asleep still wondering if the old man was right. The following day the decision would be made for all of them.

$\star$ $\star$ $\star$

'Riders comin', Ma! Riders comin'.'

It was Josh's unbroken voice that roused him from a troubled sleep. He slid out of the bed, pulled on his pants and shirt and went to the window. Two horsemen were coming down the slight rise to the north of the farm. Outside, Tommy and Josh were hoeing the small flower garden that had become their mother's pride and joy since the spring. Walter, he remembered, would be in town all day.

Beth, wiping her hands on her pinafore, hurried out to greet the strangers. McCabe watched from the bedroom window as the two men pulled up alongside Tommy.

'Is your pa home, kid?'

'No, but — ' Before he could say any more the two men had dismounted and thrust the reins of their horses towards Tommy and Josh.

'Water the horses, son, while we talk to this little lady.'

'That's my mother, mister; her name's Mrs Kane.'

The man chuckled humourlessly. 'Then we'll talk to Mrs Kane.'

The voice was like a trigger in McCabe's brain. He knew instantly that

19

he had heard it before. But where? And when?

From behind the curtains he continued to study the two men. Both were tall and slim and both had a look of meanness in their faces. The one who had spoken was dark-featured with long, black, unkempt hair and an untrimmed moustache below a long beak-like nose. His companion, fair and slightly thicker-set and a few years younger, stood back chewing on a length of straw.

'Boy says your husband ain't home,' said the first man, pushing his way past Beth and peering inside the house. Then he walked back out on the veranda and back into McCabe's view.

'Mebbe you can help then, lady. We're looking for a friend of ours — thought he might have passed by this way. Been any strangers around? He looks a bit like this.'

He unfolded a bill he had taken from his shirt and thrust it in front of Beth's face.

McCabe froze. Was it the same poster? The same Wanted bill? Were they looking for him?

Beth examined the poster and then turned away nervously.

'Nobody's been out here in weeks. You're the first visitors we've had all spring.'

The man folded the paper and placed it inside his pocket.

'That so? Then in that case you won't mind if me an' Frank here come inside. Been ridin' all night and could do with a bite to eat if it's not too much trouble.'

Without waiting, he brushed Beth aside for the second time. Frank threw down his straw and followed the older man into the house, his spurs jangling as they scraped along the floorboards.

By now they were out of McCabe's view, but he knew what he had to do. He knew who — or what — these men were. Bounty hunters. Guns for hire. And they were out to get him, of that he was certain.

Outside, Tommy and Josh, unsuspecting of any imminent danger, were brushing down the two tired horses as they took their fill of water from the trough.

McCabe crept across the room to where his gunbelt was still hanging behind the door. He was aware that the slightest sound would alert the two men in the next room. Surprise was his best weapon. The men thought Beth was alone in the house and they had to go on thinking that until he was ready to let them know differently.

Easing his Colt from its holster, he checked that it was still fully loaded — Pop might have been cautious enough to empty the chambers. Straining to hear the voices from the next room, McCabe slowly turned the handle and tried to peer through the crack between the door and the frame in an effort to figure out the positions of the two men. One of them — the fair-haired younger of the two — had his back to the bedroom door. The other was out of sight, but McCabe sensed he was close to Beth.

'What kinda man would leave a pretty lady like you all alone at home?' he was saying. 'I mean — maybe it's lucky we came along, don't you think, Frank? Stop the lady bein' lonely an' all.'

'You could be right, Ned — '

But he got no further. Gun in hand at the ready, McCabe flung open the door and stepped into the room.

'That's enough, Miller!' he snapped, waving the Colt at the man close to Beth.

The man's jaw dropped. Then he smiled, a cold, cheerless smile.

'Well, would you believe it, Frank? The little lady was lying to us. No callers she said, but here he is, the man himself, hiding away in a closet like some frightened rabbit.'

McCabe ignored the jibe.

'Just unbuckle your belts and drop them on the floor. Then get on your horses and ride out of here.'

The cheerless smile returned.

'Now, you know we can't do that, partner. An' you know why we're here, so you won't be expecting us to walk away.'

Suddenly, Ned, the smiling man, went for his gun but McCabe was ready. He fired first. The bullet ripped into the other man's chest and he slumped back against the table.

To McCabe's left, the one called Frank reached for his gun but he never made it before seeing that he was staring down the barrel of McCabe's Colt.

'Don't be a fool, young'un. Do yourself a favour, drop the belt and stay alive.'

Reluctantly, Frank unbuckled his gunbelt and let it slide to the floor. McCabe returned his attention to Ned who was writhing on the floor. He moved over and knelt beside the wounded man.

'You made a big mistake coming in here, fella. I'm giving you a chance to ride out with nothing worse than you've already got.' Waving his gun at the man called Frank he said, 'Get him up and outa here. Nearest doc is twenty miles away so if you want your friend here to live I suggest you help him into his saddle.'

Through all this, Beth Kane stood horrified at the sight of a stranger oozing blood over her kitchen floor while the man she knew as Ben McCabe stood grim-faced and cold-eyed and ruthlessly ordered the stricken man from the house.

Slowly, Frank helped the other man to his feet and, with McCabe's gun trained on the pair, helped him out of the house.

Outside, the two boys, stunned by the sound of a gunshot, had stopped in the middle of their garden work and, like their mother, looked on in horror as one of the strangers helped the other into the saddle. The man was bleeding badly and Ben was holding a gun on him.

'What's happened?' Josh whispered.

'Sshh!' Tom didn't know, but something serious was going on. Ben looked angry and he had never seen him like this before. The brothers stepped back as the men rode slowly away from the house, one of them slumped across the saddle while the other held the reins.

Satisfied that the two men, now unarmed, were well on their way, McCabe went back inside the house. Beth was slumped in a chair at the kitchen table, her head in her hands. She was crying.

Ben moved over to put a comforting arm round her shoulder but she shook herself free. Finally she got to her feet, wiped her eyes and faced him.

'Who *are* you? Those men . . . they came for you. And you knew them.'

McCabe shook his head.

'No! I don't.'

Beth was close to snapping. 'You called one of them by his name: Miller. You knew him and he knew you. Maybe Pop is right. *You are a killer*.' Then, she reached inside her pinafore pocket and pulled out a sheet of paper which she thrust into his hands.

He unfolded the paper. It was another bill poster and there again, staring back at him, was a sketch he had seen before. His own face. But this time the wording was different. It read: WANTED — DEAD OR ALIVE. FOR ROBBERY AND MURDER. $2,000 REWARD. Then came the face and below it the name: JEFF BANNER.

★ ★ ★

Old Walter had a sleepless night but it was nothing to do with an attack of insomnia. Staying awake had been a matter of choice.

Across the room the two boys slept soundly in their bunks; beyond the wall no sound had come for more than an hour as Beth breathed evenly in a peaceful sleep. At the other end of the house the man they all knew as Ben McCabe was in his room.

Still fully clothed, Walter slid out of his bed, pulled on his boots and crept across the room. He opened the door silently, making his way out to the barn at the side of the house.

Fifteen minutes later he returned, but instead of going back to his own room he stopped at McCabe's door. Without knocking he went inside. McCabe was awake, lying on his back, his hands behind his head as he stared into the darkness.

'Come in, Pop,' he said without turning his head. 'I've been wondering when you'd come.'

The old man closed the door behind him gently. The only light in the room came from the moon in a clear night sky. But it was enough.

'You know why I'm here,' Pop said, keeping his voice to little more than a whisper.

McCabe hoisted himself up and sat on the edge of the bed. He waited for the old man to continue.

'Beth told me what happened today

while I was in town. I want you out of here. Tonight.'

'She told you everything?' It was a question.

'All I need to know,' said Pop aggressively. 'Two men came here. They knew you. And you knew at least one of them. The one you shot was Ned Miller.'

Before McCabe could offer any protest, Walter hurried on, 'Look, McCabe — or Banner — or whatever your name is, you may have fooled Beth and the boys with all that memory loss, but you ain't fooled me. Not for one minute.

'You knew Ned Miller — Beth said you even called him by his name before you plugged him.'

'Listen, Pop, I — '

'No, McCabe, you listen to me and you listen good. This goes against my better judgement, but I'm giving you the chance to get out. While I was in town today I went in and had a word with the sheriff.

'I told him there was a man out at the house who we found a few weeks back with a bullet in him and I told him that this man had a price on his head.'

He paused and waited for McCabe's reaction. Then he went on, 'If you're the man you say you are, you'll get out tonight. For the sake of Beth and the boys.

'You were knocking hard on Hell's door when those boys found you in the creek, then Beth and me — we patched you up. All you've done to pay us back is bring grief and guns to this house.'

There was a short silence before McCabe said, 'This man, Ned Miller. I-I admit I know him . . . from somewhere. But I swear I can't remember where. Is he a bounty hunter?'

Pop scoffed at the question.

'Like I said, McCabe, you ain't foolin' me with all this stuff. Everybody in the territory has heard of Ned Miller. Sure he's a bounty hunter, a gun for hire, but he wasn't always that. He was a lawman up in Kansas and then Cheyenne way, town called Charlsburg until he was accused of rigging a trial . . . but you would know all about that.'

McCabe shook his head.

'Charlsburg, out of Cheyenne, you say? Maybe that's where I should start looking if I want to find out who I am.'

'I don't care where you go — so long as it's far from Beth and her sons. You've been here best part of a month now and you've overstayed your welcome. I've saddled you a horse: you can be gone before sun up — before the law gets here. And before Beth can try to stop you.'

'Looks like I don't have a choice, does it, Pop?'

Should he leave? Or should he stay to prove his innocence? But was he innocent? It is true that he vaguely recognized the man called Ned Miller. Had it been a lucky guess that he was a bounty hunter? It was obvious from Miller's rection that the two had met before. But where? Was it Charlsburg?

McCabe tried again to remember something of his past but little would come.

After a long silence, he said, 'Mebbe you're right, Pop. It's time to move out. I'm not going to find out who I am around here, that's for sure. But I tell you this, old-timer, I am not fooling. I don't know whether I'm McCabe, or Banner, or go by some other name: all I got is those posters.'

The old man reached inside his pocket. 'And this.' He opened his palm and revealed a bullet. 'It's the one we took out of your chest that first day.'

'And I never did thank you for saving my life,' said McCabe.

'All the thanks I need is you riding out of here.'

Pop tossed the bullet towards McCabe who caught it, looked it over and then placed it in his shirt pocket.

It would be a permanent reminder of how he had been saved from death by a horse doctor.

'I'll be on my way just as soon as I've

cleaned up. But I can promise you this, Pop, I'll be back just as soon as I've cleared my name and sorted out the whole goddamn mess.'

3

Frank Beckman dismounted and helped his injured friend from his saddle.

The wounded man spluttered, slumped to the ground and tried to settle against the rocks where the two men had stopped to rest.

The sun was up and the ride from the Kane farm had been slow and difficult. Twice Miller had been in danger of falling from his horse, saved each time only when Beckman had been quick enough to spot the danger. Even after they had settled down for the night, Miller had been restless, groaning through fitful bouts of sleep and being forced to sip water as sweat oozed from his pained body.

'Easy, Ned. You gotta rest up while I get you a doctor.'

Miller coughed violently. 'Too late for

that, Frank. I ain't gonna make it past midday.'

'Sure you are, Ned. I'll ride into town and bring the doctor out here — he'll soon fix you up.'

Ned Miller slowly shook his head. 'Look, Frank, we've been partners a while and I always did well by you, didn't I?'

'Sure you did, Ned, and you will do it again — '

Miller held up his hand. 'Well, now I want you to do something for me.' His voice was little more than a whisper and Beckman had to lean forward to catch what the other man was trying to say. He knew he was right. He was dying and no doctor could change that.

'I want you — I want you to get that man for me. His name ain't Jeff Banner; it's Ben McCabe and I want' — he coughed again, blood spurting from his lips — 'I want him dead, Frank. Like me. I want him dead. Like me.'

Those were Ned Miller's last words.

Frank Beckman rose to his feet and gazed towards the west. Now he was a man alone — a man with a mission . . . to kill the man he knew as Jeff Banner.

'I promise you, Ned. I'll get him for you. Whatever his name is, he ain't gonna live much longer to tell anybody. That's a promise.'

★　★　★

McCabe paused just once in his ride away from the Kane farm and when he turned in the saddle and peered back into the pre-dawn darkness he thought he caught sight of Tommy waving from one of the windows. Eventually he had to face the fact that it was only a trick of the shadows and wishful thinking on his part. Nobody in the house, except for old Walter who had followed him out to the barn and checked that he was leaving, would be awake to notice his departure.

A long ride lay ahead and now was

not the time for regrets or making plans beyond his arrival in the town of Charlsburg. What would he find there? Would he be recognized as Ben McCabe or Jeff Banner, murderer and bank robber?

He thought back to yesterday and the two unwelcome visitors, Frank and the man he had recognized as Ned Miller; the man whose name he had known in an instant. He was sure of that. He had known the name and the face.

A name and a face. Nothing else. No recollection of where or when they had met.

But that recognition was at least a start to his recovery — a link to his past life. Before that there was nothing, but now here was a connection — bounty hunter and former lawman Ned Miller and the town of Charlsburg.

★   ★   ★

The man called Frank Beckman had made a promise and he intended to keep it — not just for the $2,000 reward, but he owed Ned Miller who had helped him out of many a hole during their partnership.

He had teamed up with Miller as a hot-headed Irish kid whose temper had got him into trouble with the law more than once. The third time he had been arrested it was Miller, then a lawman, who had thrown him into jail following a drunken brawl in which a man had died. The dead man, an ageing miner, was one of the town's popular older characters and his death had riled the locals to such an extent that there was even drunken talk of a lynch mob heading for the jail.

But before they could reach the jailhouse and before the young Irish drifter could face what would have been a mockery of a trial, Miller had set him free. Said he reminded him of himself when he was nothing more than a kid.

Beckman left town in a hurry, but within a week he was sharing a bottle in a small-town saloon with Miller. He had been stripped of his lawman's badge after a man he thought was a friend sold him out over a few private deals he had set up. Beckman never learned what those deals were and he knew better than to ask. If Ned had wanted him to know he would have told him.

But now Ned was dead; their partnership was over and he had a promise to keep.

He placed the last rock on the shallow makeshift grave he had dug for his friend. He did not know whether Ned had ever been religious but he, as an Irishman, had been brought up to believe in the existence of God so he had added a wooden cross in which he had carved the name Ned Miller. He turned away from the grave after muttering his way through a brief badly remembered prayer, put on his Stetson against the climbing sun and walked over to where his horse was grazing. He mounted up, jerked the reins causing the animal to snort a mild protest and headed back towards the Kane farm. If McCabe was still there he would carry out his promise. If not, he could force the woman or one of her kids to tell him where the man had gone. And he wouldn't be quite as squeamish as Ned would have been if he had to force the information out of any of them.

The temper that had got Frank Beckman into a lot of trouble in his youth was rising again and, as he dug his heels viciously into his horse, he had no intention of trying to control it.

He rode hard and long, pausing only to give his horse some much needed water, and there was still some daylight left when the small farmhouse came into view. But it was fading fast and he decided to wait until darkness enveloped the house before making his move.

Riding in as close as he felt was possible without fear of detection, he dismounted and tied his tired horse to a nearby bush. He tried to picture in his mind the layout of the house as he remembered it from his brief visit the previous day. The main room was at the front, kitchen to the side with two, or maybe three, other rooms where the family slept.

Right now he reckoned they would be eating their evening meal, all around the table in the main room. If he burst in, he would catch them unaware, unarmed and open to the persuasion of a gun.

He settled down and waited . . .

Beckman had been right about the way things stood inside the house. Beth was serving up supper to the boys and Pop who were sitting in silence around the large table.

It had been a subdued day in the Kane household. First the two boys had risen early, eager to join Ben out in the fields as they had done for the past few days.

Pop said nothing to dampen their enthusiasm for the day ahead until Beth appeared to prepare the breakfasts.

'Only three of us today, Beth,' Pop

informed her, as she wrapped her pinafore around her and readied herself for the first meal of the day. 'Ben already out there — without eating?' she asked, surprised.

Pop hesitated only briefly before conveying his news. 'I wanted you all here before I told you — he's gone.'

Puzzled, Tommy and Josh looked at each other. Beth stopped what she was doing and waited for the old man to continue.

'I told him he had to go,' said Pop. 'He rode out before dawn.' He was not prepared to offer any further explanation, considering the matter closed, but the two young brothers wanted to know more.

Eventually he relented. 'I told him he wasn't welcome here. We didn't need his kind — '

'His kind?' Beth interrupted. 'What's his kind, Pop?'

'You know what I mean, Beth. He's a wanted man. He's running from the law and those two men you told me about who came when I was in town, well, sounds to me like they was bounty hunters. And bounty hunters spell trouble. Besides, you told me he shot one of them.'

'To save me and the boys!' she protested. 'To save us.'

'He did it to save his own hide, can't you see? I told you he was no good and now he's proved it. I never did believe that story of his about losing his memory an' all. Now he's run out again, and one day the law will catch up with him. You should be pleased that he'll be many miles away from here when that happens.'

'You had no right to send him away, Pop. No right at all! This is my house and I say who stays here. Erskine . . . ' She faltered but quickly regained her power of speech. 'Erskine was my husband, but he's not here any more. You got to accept that, Pop.'

Walter Kane rose slowly but deliberately from the table and stared her in the face before he strode purposefully from the room, slamming the door behind him.

He spent the rest of the day in isolation out in the fields while the two boys confined themselves to their room and their studies. Beth was left to wonder whether she would ever again see Ben McCabe, the man whom she hoped might one day follow Erskine Kane into her bed.

Now the silence at the end of the day only emphasized the rift between Walter Kane and his son's widow, with the grandsons still wondering what Ben had done that was so bad he had to ride off into the night without saying goodbye.

Despite the discord the evening meal was Beth's usual tasty fare but the circumstances made it far from the most pleasant the family had shared.

Pop had made another effort to break through the icy atmosphere with a suggestion that they all should go into town the next morning — a treat for the boys and an opportunity for Beth to meet up with friends and visit the stores.

The idea was greeted with a grunt of approval from the boys and a shrug of indifference from their mother.

Frustrated, Pop tried again. 'Look, Beth, I did what I thought was right for everybody. That man — '

He got no further. Suddenly the door burst open and a man brandishing a rifle stood in the open doorway, silhouetted against the darkening night sky. He had made no attempt to hide his identity and Beth recognized him instantly as one of the two men who had been at the house the previous day.

Pop stood up from the table and moved towards the gunman.

'Stay back, old man! You' — he waved the rifle at Beth — 'where is he? Where's Banner?'

'Banner? Who — ?'

'Don't play dumb with me, lady. He was here yesterday. He put a bullet in my partner and now he's dead. So tell me where he is, unless you want the same thing for one of your boys here.'

Frank Beckman switched his attention to young Josh.

'You, kid — get over here.'

The younger brother rose from his chair and moved to obey the order but his grandfather grabbed his arm.

'Stay there, Josh. Look, mister, if it's the man we know as Ben McCabe you're after, he's gone. He ain't here.'

Frank stiffened. His temper was rising and Pop could sense it.

'This isn't our fight. You've got no quarrel with us.'

'Where is he?' Frank snapped. 'Tell me, or . . . ' He raised his rifle and pointed it at Josh's head.

Pop stepped in front of the boy who was now cowering in his seat.

'He's heading out up Cheyenne way. He left here before dawn today. He's long gone but Charlsburg's where you'll find him.'

Frank Beckman lowered his gun but promptly raised it again. He was agitated, confused. He had come to this

God-forsaken farm to get the man who had killed his partner and now . . .

'You ain't foolin' with me, old man? Cos if you are — '

'He's not fooling. He's telling you the truth.' It was Beth who had stepped in. 'I'm sorry about your friend, but we can't do anything to help.'

Frank spun to face her. 'You ain't half as sorry as Banner or McCabe is gonna to be when I catch up with him.'

'What you gonna do, mister? You gonna kill us?'

'Tommy!' Beth moved across the floor and pulled her elder son close. Beckman looked long and hard at the young boys.

'If your ma and the old-timer here's tellin' the truth you ain't gonna have a problem from me, kid. But, if they're lyin' you'd better believe it — I'll be back.'

Without another word he backed slowly out of the doorway and hurried off to where he had tethered his horse. Charlsburg. That was where it all started and that was where it would end.

'I promised you I'd finish him, Ned and I'm on my way,' he said aloud, turning his mount away from the farmhouse and into the night.

Inside the house, Pop was comforting Beth who had broken down in tears.

★ ★ ★

McCabe was surprised to find that he was able to follow the trail as if he knew it like the palm of his hand.

Two stops at tiny, unmapped and, as far as he could tell, unnamed townships passed off without incident, but on the third night he got the impression that he was the subject of some inquisitive looks from fellow drinkers in the small, smoke-filled saloon. But he was never approached or challenged so he was able to put the feeling of unease down to nothing more than the fact that a stranger — any stranger — would be a curiosity around those parts.

By the fourth night, after a comfortable stay in one of the better hotels around he was ready to face up to the ride into Charlsburg and learn what was in store for him there.

As he mounted up after a hearty breakfast he couldn't help but hope that the first somebody who recognized him wasn't one of those eager to put another bullet in him and collect the reward.

4

The large room at the back of the main street hotel was crowded with noisy, fist-shaking cattlemen. Up on the platform Mitchell Dredge rose to his full height, spread his bulky frame and tried to call for order. The cattlemen were angry at the news they had just been given by the pompous Dredge, chief spokesman and district manager of the railroad. The cost of transporting their prize stock had risen beyond all their expectations.

'Gentlemen! Gentlemen!' He tried desperately to regain control of the situation. 'The new prices merely help to cover the railroad company's increasing costs — '

His call for reason was drowned in the racket of jeers from the protesting cattle owners. Close by, the stockyards were crammed with steers ready for shipment first to Cheyenne, then out East and from there eventually to the restaurant tables of the major cities.

Now, after several weeks on the trail bringing their beef to the railroad yard ready for the final leg of their journey to the slaughterhouses, they had been informed that the cost of continuing the journey would cut deeply into their profits from the sales.

Dredge could see he was losing the battle for order and the cattle breeders were in no mood to listen to any more platitudes.

He knew that eventually calm would be restored and they would reluctantly pay the extra costs he was demanding. Short of seizing the train there was little else they could do to get their cattle across the hundreds of miles.

It was only a matter of holding his nerve. His feigned sympathies with the cattlemen over the price rises which he claimed had come from head office — showing them a faked document to add conviction to his display of shared concern — would get him through what he knew would be a difficult situation. By the time the big shots behind their oak desks had realized what was happening, he would be well out of town and out of Wyoming altogether and living the good life out West in California.

Dredge had been in this sort of situation before and his wits had got him out of any impending trouble. He had spent the last three years running the office his way and in the past year that meant for every dollar that went into the railroad's account one would find its way into the pocket of the district manager.

But maybe he had been getting careless and it was time to move on after this latest racket. The danger signs had first started when the company brought in that agent. They had said he had been sent in to help him solve and clean up a string of robberies that had plagued the railroad. But Dredge knew better — the man was a company spy.

It had needed a lot of cunning and money to get him out of his hair once and for all. It had been an expensive narrow escape, but it had been money well spent and the spy had gone for good. Framing the man for murder and robbery had been one of his better ideas.

All that was needed now was to get this latest consignment of cattle on its way and the payments in his own private safe. He listened to the cattlemen arguing among themselves. It was time to leave the hall.

Dredge nodded to one of his underlings, a silent instruction to carry on with the meeting while he returned to the office to prepare for the inevitable bitterness when the traders eventually came to pay their bills.

Outside, Dredge did not immediately head for the office. Instead he made his way towards a small saloon on the opposite side of the street. He waved and smiled pleasantly at the man on the desk, headed up the circular staircase and without knocking entered the second room along the passage.

The woman, a slim redhead, was folding a green dress and placing it alongside several others already packed into the bag on the bed.

Dredge rested his hands on her shoulders and she turned slowly to prepare herself for the obligatory embrace. He kissed her lightly on the tip of her nose and backed away.

Mitchell Dredge knew that Carla Blake's charms were only available because he was a meal ticket away from life as a saloon singer — and worse. He wasn't foolish enough to think that this was a love match although he hoped that time — and California — might change that.

'Almost done, darling?' he asked, smiling and running his finger lightly down her cheek. 'And you haven't said anything to the others?'

'Of course not. You said we had to keep our plans a secret.' She chuckled. 'But you never said why. Are you going to tell me?'

'It's best you don't know everything,' he said, with a hint of edginess in his voice. 'All you have to do is make sure you're ready when I bring the carriage to the back of the hotel tonight. Then we'll be well on our way to Laramie by this time tomorrow.'

Carla sighed. 'And then on to California.' They kissed and Dredge left his woman to complete the task of filling her bag with everything she could pack into it. Downstairs he stopped at the bar for a whiskey before stepping out into the afternoon sunlight.

He stopped on the boardwalk and was adjusting his hat to shield his eyes when he spotted the lone rider coming down the middle of Main Street. He froze to the spot. It couldn't be! Not him! He was dead! He had paid to make sure of that. But now he was back and Dredge knew there could be only one reason. He quickly ducked back into the shadows of the hotel and waited for the rider to pass. He stood there for what seemed like an age before the newcomer, staring straight ahead, slowly led his horse towards the livery yard at the corner of the street.

A mixture of panic and fear was setting in for Dredge who hurried into the safety of the hotel bar. He ordered another whiskey and emptied the glass in one swallow.

The barman noticed the look of anxiety on Dredge's face as he refilled the railroad boss's glass.

'You all right, Mr Dredge?' The concerned question seemed to go unheard, so he tried again.

'Huh?'

'You all right? You look as though you've seen a ghost.'

Mitchell Dredge tried to chuckle, but made no other response. He slapped his empty glass on the bar top and headed for the staircase. Up in the room Carla was sitting at the mirror putting the finishing touches to her hair. The return of her lover caught her by surprise not only in mid-action but also mid-thought.

She put down her comb and forced a welcoming smile — a smile that did not match her innermost thoughts of the man who was now leaning over her and wearing a worried look. She sensed that something was wrong but she wasn't prepared for his news.

'We've got to change our plans,' he said, a note of alarm — or was it simply fear? — in his voice. 'We can't wait until tonight. Be outside the back of the hotel in an hour.'

'An hour? Why? What's happened?'

'Just be there — and be ready to leave!' he snapped. 'I've got things to do.'

He turned, and without another word, hurried out of the room.

Immediately, Carla was on her feet. She went to the door, opened it slightly and listened for his heavy footsteps fading away along the corridor and down the staircase. As soon as she was sure that Dredge had left the building, she pulled her light cloak from its peg behind the door and hurried along the passageway. But instead of following him down to the front of the hotel she went along to the door at the end of the passage. She knew it led to a storeroom and from there to an outside flight of steps at the rear of the hotel where she was due to meet up with him again an hour later. Before that she, just like the crooked railroad boss, 'had things to do' and they included getting an urgent message to the man who would be replacing Mitchell Dredge somewhere on the road to Laramie.

Jay Munroe would have to be told of the change of plans. Luckily she knew exactly where to find him at that time of day. His favourite card table was only a short walk down the back street.

Leaving the hotel, Dredge scoured the sunbaked streets for any sign of the man whose arrival had filled him with a mix of fear and confusion. Maybe his eyes had been playing him tricks in the blinding sun. McCabe was dead: Munroe had killed him. He had seen him die — a bullet to the head and another to the chest to make certain. And he had collected the $2,000 reward, a bonus paid out of Dredge's own pocket.

He said he had followed him for three days before the chance came. Why hadn't Dredge insisted on seeing the body? He should have stood firm even when Munroe told him about the two kids who had been fishing along the stream and just happened to come along at the wrong time.

Had they heard the shots? Probably not, Munroe explained, they were just a couple of kids fishing and they would hear gunfire all the time and thought it was some old-timer out shooting for his dinner. And Munroe argued that he wasn't the only one chasing McCabe after Dredge had put out those phoney Wanted bills on a trumped-up murder and robbery charge.

True, that had been one of Dredge's better ideas. Stage a robbery and the killing of some stockyard no-account while McCabe was heading out of town on some family business and then put the idea about that McCabe had been seen hightailing it out of town when Dredge himself turned up at the stockyard to find the old man dead and the cash gone.

But now here he was . . . not dead as Munroe had said . . . but back in town and Dredge knew that he was looking for him.

Dredge had trusted Munroe, they had worked together often before, ever since Carla had introduced them at one of those cattlemen's conventions. But now he had failed him — the man the rail company had sent to spy on him was back.

First he had to see Munroe, to tell him that he'd failed, tell him that he still had to earn that $2,000; tell him that McCabe was in town.

Another glance along the street assured him that it was safe to step out from the boardwalk and head for the one place he knew Munroe would be. He had to hurry . . . time was short and he still had to empty the railroad company safe without being seen. Fortunately, he expected the arguments over the price rises would go on for some time so the office would be deserted at least until the angry crowds broke up.

Ignoring the friendly greetings from the few neighbours he passed on the street, Dredge hurried past the general store, barber shop and bank before pushing open the batwing doors and entering the semi-darkened smoke-filled room of the Silver Lady saloon.

He stopped in his tracks. Munroe was there . . . and he was talking to Carla. They both looked agitated.

Neither of them saw him enter the room and he was about to go across to where they were standing next to the small platform that served as a stage for the dancing girls when something held him back.

Munroe put his arm around Carla's shoulder and led her through a heavy curtain at the side of the stage. What were they up to? Why were they acting so furtively?

Dredge looked around the room. Nobody was taking any notice of him. Edging his way forward, he crept along the side of the piano and reached the point where he could clearly hear their whispering.

It was Carla who was speaking urgently. 'I don't know why we're leaving in an hour but it changes everything. What are we going to do?'

Munroe appeared to think for a moment before replying, 'Can't you keep him here longer? Maybe an extra hour. That would give me the chance to get out there and pick him off like a rabbit — just like we planned.'

It was Carla's turn to think long and hard before replying, 'I-I don't know. He could get suspicious, if I — '

'Come on . . . you know how to get round the old goat. You've done it many times before.'

'Jay, you know how much I hate him touching me: it's you I'm thinking of all the time, why do I . . . ' She fell silent and Dredge was left to guess what was happening behind the curtain. It did not need much of an imagination. They were in cahoots and had been playing him for a fool.

He did not have to hear any more. Slowly he backed away and left the saloon. There was no time to waste. Ignoring the notion that he might be walking straight into more danger in the form of Ben McCabe, Mitchell Dredge made his way towards the railroad office. It was, as he had expected, totally deserted. Dragging his satchel from its hiding place beneath his desk, he knelt in front of the safe. There was no time to count the money, no time to regret that he would not be able to fill his pockets with the cash that would come from the increased levy he had planned to take from the cattlemen; instead it was the time for action.

He stuffed the notes into his bag, then with a swift swish of his arm, he scattered the papers from his desk all over the room, pulled a cabinet down so it crashed to the floor and then, taking his gun, smashed the door window and lock. The evidence of a break-in complete, he made his way along to the stable yard, gave the ostler instructions to saddle his horse and then waited nervously, sensing that at any moment somebody would walk by and wonder why he was there.

But nobody came. Mitchell Dredge mounted up, threw the stuffed satchel across the saddle and spun the horse out through the gate and into the street. It was then that a tall figure stepped off the boardwalk and straight into the path of the horse.

Instinctively, Dredge pulled on the reins, drawing the chestnut to a sudden stop. He stared down into the face of the man he had almost knocked to the ground.

The man stared back up and their eyes met.

'Easy, mister, don't be in such a goddamn hurry.'

Dredge felt the sweat oozing from every pore.

'I — er — '

'No harm done. Just take it easy next time.'

Mitchell Dredge couldn't speak. He just turned the horse away, dug in his heels and headed the animal out into the sun. He was well clear of the town boundary when he had to stop to catch his breath.

What had happened? Why was he still alive and riding out with maybe $20,000 in his saddle-bag? Why hadn't Ben McCabe known him and dragged him out of the saddle?

5

McCabe shrugged his shoulders. The rider who had almost knocked him off his feet rode away without a second look and no apology. It was strange, as though the man was about to say something but then changed his mind. Was there a look of fear in his eyes? Was his face familiar?

McCabe dismissed the incident from his mind, he had far more important things to think about and he knew that the next few minutes would be crucial.

He was on his way to the sheriff's office and, once there, there would be no going back. He had learned that the lawman in Charlsburg was new and apparently an honest man. His name was Brad Nicholls, but that meant nothing. No helpful bells, no triggers in the brain. Nothing.

McCabe pushed open the office door

and entered the room. A man about McCabe's age and height was sitting behind a wide desk in the middle of the office. He was deeply engrossed in a mound of papers and did not even look up as McCabe approached the desk.

'Hold on, mister,' he said, continuing to thumb through the pages.

'No hurry, Sheriff. I know the feeling.'

What made him say that? He didn't know the feeling — or did he? Did the expression really mean something?

The lawman eventually threw back his head and sighed.

'Ah, that lot can wait — what can I do for you, mister?'

This was the test. This moment, when Sheriff Brad Nicholls looked into the face of the man who believed he was Ben McCabe — or Jeff Banner — or some other name that he had yet to hear.

McCabe hestitated, hoping — or perhaps dreading — that there would be a hint of recognition from the man with the badge. None came.

'Do you know me, Sheriff? Do you know who I am?'

Nicholls supressed a chuckle. 'Well, if you don't know, mister, I don't think I can help you.'

McCabe kept calm.

'No,' he returned the half-smile. 'I know me,' he lied, 'do you?'

'Sorry, stranger, I guess not. But if you've got a problem — '

'Does the name Ben McCabe mean anything to you?'

'Nope, can't say it does.'

'Jeff Banner?'

'Nope again.'

Ben McCabe was baffled. He did not know exactly what he was prepared for, but it wasn't this. The sheriff in the town where his troubles all began, where he had thought that his face and those names would be all over the wanted posters, had no idea who he was.

'You're sure?' he persisted.

Nicholls rose from his chair and

moved towards his visitor.

'Look, what is this, mister? I told you I've never heard of those fellas. Now you saw I was busy, so if you've got nothing else to ask me I'd like to get on with what I was doing.'

But McCabe refused the suggestion to leave.

'How long have you been sheriff here in Charlsburg?'

'I'm new here — no more'n three weeks.'

'And who had the job before that?'

The lawman was losing patience with the stranger. He had heard enough and from what he was hearing he didn't want to have any dealings with the man.

'Look, I don't know what this business of yours is, but if it helps you to hurry up and get out of here I can tell you that when I took this job the town had no local lawman. Before that it was a man called Ned Miller. And I didn't know him either, but folks around these parts tell me he wasn't above using the law and the badge for his own use.'

Ben McCabe felt a sudden surge of relief. Ned Miller, whose name had triggered something in his brain back at the Kane farm, had been a crooked lawman. McCabe felt himself visibly relax.

'Sheriff, have you got time to listen to a story . . . ?'

★   ★   ★

When the man had finished, Sheriff Nicholls wasn't sure whether he should be slapping this stranger into one of the vacant cells in the jailhouse at the back of the office building, or sending him on his way as some sort of eccentric drifter looking for anybody he could call a friend.

In the end he did neither. He was inclined to believe that his visitor was what he claimed to be: a victim who had no recollection of any of the crimes he was supposed to have committed. That didn't mean he wasn't guilty of them, of course, but Nicholls showed enough encouragement for the man to go on with his story.

'You don't know anything about these posters' — he unfolded the one that old Pop Kane had waved under his nose — 'or this?' He held up the one that Miller and his young friend had left on the table.

The sheriff stared at both bills.

'Ben McCabe. Jeff Banner. Same face. Same reward. Same crimes — robbery and murder. And both pictures of you. And somebody put up this two-thousand-dollar reward — it wasn't this town, I can tell you that.'

'It's like I said,' Ben reminded him, 'and right now I'm getting more convinced that I'm being hunted down for something I didn't do.' He paused before a sudden thought prompted him to go on.

'If the law didn't put up this reward, who did? Who wants to pay two thousand dollars to see me dead?'

Again the lawman shook his head. This was all before his arrival in town.

Two thousand dollars — not a fortune by any stretch but maybe enough for some trigger-happy drunk to try his luck on an unsuspecting man.

'Maybe I can ask around?' he suggested.

'I can do that myself,' Ben protested, but Nicholls just smiled.

'And suppose one of those folk you are asking just happens to be handy with a six-gun and in need of two thousand dollars? Before you've figured it out, I'll be calling for the undertaker to move you off the street. I suggest you keep out of sight for a day or two. That's as long as I'll need to find out where these came from' — he waved the posters at McCabe — 'and maybe I'll find out if you're telling the truth.'

McCabe nodded. 'I hope I am, Sheriff. Because if I'm not that would put us on opposite sides and I reckon neither of us would want that.'

★ ★ ★

Carla Blake stood at the foot of the steps at the back of the hotel and waited. Her baggage was packed and waiting to be loaded on to the rig when Dredge eventually turned up. She started to pace up and down along the narrow back street before eventually reaching the conclusion that he wouldn't be coming at all. She had no idea that Mitchell Dredge was several miles out of town trying to recover from the shock that the man he had reason to fear most in the whole world was still alive.

* * *

Dredge poured another shot of whiskey down his throat, but it did little to ease the panic that had set in ever since he ran into McCabe that morning. He cursed Munroe for his incompetence and he cursed himself for his failure to make sure that the job had been done before paying Munroe his bonus.

For almost a year he had been the

brains behind their small profitable outfit while Munroe, that crooked lawman Miller and his young sidekick had been his workforce. It had been successful because Dredge, with his inside knowledge, knew where and when to hit the trains and the stages carrying the rich pickings. This is how Munroe repaid him — by failing to see off that meddling railroad agent McCabe.

McCabe had been a thorn in his side since the day of his arrival at Charlsburg. Sure, he had acted friendly enough, saying that he was only there to help clean up the mess left by a string of robberies that had been plaguing the rail company and their stage-coach branch for so long.

Dredge poured himself another drink. Did McCabe think he was stupid? Did he really think that Mitchell Dredge couldn't see that he was the man under suspicion?

He was getting close. It was time to move on with one last big pay day. The chance came when McCabe told him that he was leaving town on family business and would be gone for a few days. The timing was perfect. Dredge would arrange to meet his bosses in Cheyenne, leaving Miller and the others to break into the office. Later, Dredge would spread stories of McCabe's hurried retreat from the scene of the robbery. And then there was the murder. The old man's killing had been unfortunate but it helped to add weight to Dredge's reasons for putting up a reward and sending out Wanted bills for the capture of McCabe dead or alive. The use of the name Jeff Banner also helped — McCabe had told him he had once used the name for an undercover operation up in Kansas. Any man using an alias would automatically come under suspicion. And Dredge was sure that the rail company did not know about McCabe's involvement in a killing while he was a young deputy. Dredge would let them know about that.

But now, because of Munroe's failure and the continued absence of Miller and the Beckman kid, Dredge was starting to panic. Which was why he was drinking more than his fill at a remote bar room in some out of the way town . . .

★　★　★

Brad Nicholls made his inquiries around the town and his questions produced a variety of answers, but by the time he had finished the mystery of the man with no memory still remained.

The sheriff's first call took him to the man who knew everybody in town, old Doc Riley.

'Sure, I know Ben McCabe — or Jeff Banner as he sometimes called himself,' said the old man.

'Huh?' Nicholls acted dumb.

It did not take Doc long to warm to his subject. 'He's some sort of detective working for the railroad. He's Ben McCabe around these parts, but he was

Banner when he worked out of Kansas. He told me it was company policy for its agents to work under different aliases in different areas. Harder to trace when the bad guys came calling; used to joke about it.'

'What about the robbery at the railroad? And the killing of that old watchman?' Nicholls pressed the medical man.

'Fah!' Doc Riley let out a scornful sneer. 'They're saying Ben did that? Let me tell you, Brad, McCabe is an honest man who would never betray a trust. As for gunning down old Jed, it was only a week before that Ben had saved his life when he snatched him from a runaway horse. He even got the old man the job. He thought a lot of the old-timer.'

'Then why did he go missing the night of the robbery?'

'Who says he did go missing?' Riley snapped.

'Well, I hear he hasn't been seen since that night — and there's some twenty thousand dollars gone, too.'

The doctor poured himself an extra cup of coffee and studied his visitor. Did Brad Nicholls really believe that McCabe was a killer? And why now? What had prompted this sudden interest?

'There must be some other reason, some explanation for Ben's so-called disappearance. They tell me I'm a good judge of character, Brad, and if that holds, I can tell you Ben McCabe is no thief, and he's no cold-hearted killer. I'd stake my life on that.'

Sheriff Nicholls touched his hat, smiled and rose from his chair. 'I'm sure he would be glad to hear you say that, Doc.'

Doc Riley sipped more coffee. 'Yes, I'm sure he would, if only we knew where he was.'

* * *

The lawman made two more calls in his attempt to find out more about the mysterious Ben McCabe.

The first took him to the office of the town newspaper, the *Charlsburg Clarion* where the proprietor and editor Wilfred Wainwright added his weight to the glowing reference given by Doc Riley, but with one rider.

'Being a newspapermen I hear things, Sheriff — some true, some just malicious gossip, some a combination of both.'

Nicholls waited for the talkative Englishman to go on. He was clearly in possession of some knowledge that had not made it into the columns of his newspaper.

'Before I came to Charlsburg I owned a newspaper up in Kansas where your man McCabe was a young deputy sheriff. Seems there was some trouble in town one night and a local hothead — man by the name of Fuller — got involved in a fight over a card game.

'McCabe stepped in to break it up and the man Fuller pulled a gun on him. Somehow McCabe managed to get it away from him but in the ruckus that followed, Fuller took a bullet.'

'From McCabe?'

'That's just it,' Wainwright said eagerly. 'Nobody knows for sure. McCabe wasn't even carrying at the time and people who saw it say Fuller's gun spun away across the saloon floor during the fight.'

'So how'd it happen?' The lawman was impatient to hear the rest of the newspaperman's story, but the editor was clearly enjoying the time it was taking to re-tell the tale.

The Englishman's satisfied smile irritated Nicholls but he waited for the editor to continue.

'Nobody was prepared to speak to me for fear that I'd put their name in the newspaper, but the best guess was that Fuller had been gunned down by McCabe's boss who walked in to the saloon halfway through the fight and was watching from the doorway. It seems the local sheriff shot Fuller.'

'The sheriff, who was he?'

Again the Englishman took time to enjoy himself.

'Now that's the thing, Mr Nicholls, like McCabe he ended up here in Charlsburg. Name of Ned Miller.'

★ ★ ★

Nicholls' next call took him to the offices of the East Wyoming Mercantile Bank where the major stakeholder was Carter Brennan, one-time town mayor and its leading citizen since the days before it grew to its present size and importance as a transport centre close to the main city of Cheyenne.

Brennan was a heavy, red-faced man in his late fifties with a ready smile that was usually masked by clouds of smoke from one of his expensive cigars. The banker greeted Nicholls with the usual warm handshake he kept for the man married to his only daughter.

His opinion of Ben McCabe was, like the others, favourable, and he could no more see the man betraying a trust than, say, Brad himself. Nicholls left the office with the growing belief that

McCabe was all he claimed to be.

The lawman's final visit before he looked up McCabe again was to the Silver Lady saloon. For two reasons: he needed a drink and he needed time to think, to decide what he would do next.

Cassidy, the cheery barman, served him with his usual shot of whiskey and a beer to follow and he made his way to an empty table close to the small stage that, at this time of day, was deserted. It would stay that way until the night customers, the gamblers, the big drinkers and the womanizers looking for a saloon girl, came through the batwing doors.

Nicholls sat alone with his thoughts and his drink. What he had learned so far about the man he now knew as Ben McCabe was that the opinions of those he respected — doctor, former mayor and newspaper editor — painted a positive picture, certainly not one of a killer on the run. But he still wasn't totally convinced. The story about his connection with Ned Miller, the man he admitted he had wounded at a remote farmhouse on the other side of the state, cast doubts. Again he examined the two wanted bills bearing McCabe's face and the two names.

Two thousand dollars reward — enough to tempt any number of bounty hunters yet here was the man openly walking the streets in search of the truth about himself.

Nicholls finished his drink and made a decision . . . to trust McCabe. Any man, even one without a memory, who could walk the streets of a town where he was supposedly wanted for murder and robbery had to be crazy — or innocent. He did not think that Ben McCabe was crazy.

But his thoughts on McCabe and his troubles were interrupted when Chester Grant, a young clerk at the rail company's office, burst into the saloon. He stopped abruptly in the doorway, his eyes scouring the room until he spotted Nicholls alone at his table. He hurried over and breathlessly blurted out his message.

'Sheriff! You gotta come — quick!'

'Slow down, young fella. What's the all-fired hurry?'

'Down at the yard!' Chester gasped, still trying to recover his breath. 'The cattle owners — they're threatening to riot cos they can't get their beef loaded and they are goin' to take over the whole train!'

Brad Nicholls rose from his seat and put on his hat. 'Can't Dredge handle this? It's his job to organize the movement of the cattle, isn't it?'

'That's just it, Sheriff, I can't find Mr Dredge any place, and . . . ' His voice tailed off.

'And what Chester?'

'The office. It's been ransacked again and the safe's been emptied. All the money's gone. The money and Mr Dredge both.'

'Let's go, Chester. Looks like we might have to go find a thief as well as stop a riot.'

The pair hurried out of the saloon

into the bright sunlight. Neither had spotted the woman at the top of the stairs who had heard their conversation.

Nor did they hear the curse escape from the lips of Carla Blake.

* * *

Jay Munroe spat at the news.

'So, the old buzzard has run out on you after all,' he growled at Carla when she told him what she had overheard in the saloon. 'Looks like he's gotten away with everything.'

The woman remained calm. Inside she was seething. Not at Mitchell Dredge for running out on her — she could live with that and she always knew it would happen one day — but at Jay's all-too-quick acceptance that the old man had won.

'We can go after him, Jay. We know he's headed for Laramie. Two fast horses and we'd be on him by nightfall. If he carried out his plan he'll have some twenty thousand dollars with him.'

She leaned forward and gripped his arm. 'That can be ours, Jay — you and me.'

She studied Munroe's face. He was a handsome man. Dark-eyed, square jawed, he was clean shaven save for a neat pencil-thin moustache that partially covered a small scar to the left of his mouth. He was tall, but slim — the kind to turn a woman's head when he entered a room. But, like all the men Carla Blake had known — and there had been many even in her short adult life — he was disposable.

Perhaps that was why she tolerated him — he was a usable commodity. As a lover he was preferable to the pawing, slavering old wretch Mitchell Dredge, but then, in Carla's experience, lovers were easy to come by.

'Twenty thousand dollars, Jay,' she stressed, 'and it's waiting for us out there. You've done it before so I guess you ain't squeamish.'

Her tone suggested that she thought he might not have the stomach for such a job, and caused him to bristle.

Carla could see that he was about to weaken — again — so she pressed on. 'Dredge thought we were going off together so he told me all his plans. He won't change them now.'

'You know a lot about him.' Munroe's sardonic chuckle unsettled her but only for a moment.

'Don't be a fool, Jay. We're wasting time. If we don't catch him before he gets to Laramie we could lose him. And the money.'

Munroe finished his shot of whiskey and rose from the table. He walked across the room and stared out of the window. Twenty thousand dollars. And Carla. All he had to do was get rid of the old lecher Mitchell Dredge. There would be no witnesses on a dark road out of Laramie. From there they could head west to Utah, maybe Nevada or California. Just him and Carla, and $20,000 stake money. It would mean a break-up of their profitable little business, but most of that money had gone on cards and dice. He needed $20,000.

'Jay?'

Carla's voice broke into his thoughts. She was right. There was no time to waste. The longer they delayed the more miles Dredge would be putting between them. He turned to face her, the decision made. 'Get yourself into some riding clothes. We leave in ten minutes.'

6

Brad Nicholls did his best to settle the cattlemen's growing dispute with the rail company and peace and quiet were restored to the stockyard at Charlsburg. Soon the cattle would be loaded — at the old price — and heading for Cheyenne and all points east.

The case of the missing station manager and the money were more of a problem but even that would have to wait. Right now he figured Ben McCabe needed his attention — and the help of Doc Riley.

'The man's clearly convinced he's innocent even though he can't remember,' he told the medical man, as the pair made their way up the stairs to McCabe's hotel room.

'Don't know what I can do to help you there, Brad. Sure, I know Ben but if what you say is right he probably won't recognize me.

'Fact is, the mind's a strange thing and we don't know too much about how it works. A man could lose his memory and never get it back. Or it could come back just like that' — he snapped his fingers — 'for no reason we can figure.'

Nicholls thought about that but pressed ahead, 'Or it could come back sort of slowly?'

Riley nodded.

'Look, you were here when this robbery and killing happened. Just tell him about it. Maybe that would help.'

'I'll try, but don't hold out too much hope. Like I said, the mind can play all kinds of funny tricks that we don't understand.'

They reached the door of McCabe's room, knocked and waited. Eventually Nicholls called, 'Ben — it's me, the sheriff. I got the doc here, wants to talk.'

The door opened slowly, inch by inch, as though the man in the room had not believed what he had heard. Then he relaxed, stepped back and the two men entered the room.

'Ben, this is Doc Riley. I thought — '

'I know who he is. Hello, Doc.'

The two visitors exchanged looks of surprise.

'You know? You remember him?'

McCabe shrugged. 'I-I guess so. I've been staring out of the window since I checked in here and I started to remember things. Little things, you know — like I'd been here before.'

'Such as? What do you remember?' Riley sounded eager, like an investigator given the opportunity to explore the workings of another man's mind. He turned to the sheriff. 'I told you, the mind's a mystery to most of us. Even the best health care can't provide an answer about recovery from memory loss other than 'we'll just have to wait and see'. The fact that the brain recovers at all is seen as something of a miracle even by the best surgeons.'

Then he turned back to McCabe. 'Go on, Ben.'

'There's not much to tell,' McCabe said. 'I was looking out staring at nothing in particular when I remembered the man who had almost knocked me over when I was on my way to your office, Brad. He was in such a hurry I don't think he saw me, but he just turned and hightailed it out of town. His name came to me from nowhere: it was Mitchell Dredge and he worked for the railroad.'

Nicholls made a gesture to interrupt but Doc Riley stopped him.

'What do you remember about him, Ben — or is it Jeff Banner?'

Strangely, McCabe reacted without any sign of surprise.

'That was one of the names on the Wanted bills I showed the sheriff.'

Doc Riley nodded. 'You once told me about it. You were an agent with the railroad — said it was company policy for agents to use aliases on different jobs in different towns.'

McCabe was puzzled. 'I told you, Doc? Why would I do that?'

Riley suddenly changed his line. 'How's your leg?'

'My leg? What about my leg?'

'I had to fix it up for you when your horse fell on you. That's when you got all friendly and talkative about your job. Don't you remember?'

McCabe thought for a moment, trying to rack his brain, forcing it into remembering the incident. Nothing came.

He shook his head. 'Sorry, Doc. But this man Dredge, why should I remember that name?'

Again the medical man interrupted. 'You told me the rail company were getting suspicious about him and you were sent up from — Kansas, I recall — to investigate what was going on here and in Cheyenne.

'Seems there was a break-in at the office and an old cleaner was killed during the robbery. Dredge was supposedly away on business someplace and when he got back you were missing. Or, at least you weren't where you should have been. Word got round that the only explanation for your disappearance was that you were the robber; the one who gunned down the old man. That's when Dredge said he persuaded the rail company to put up the reward money and sent out the names of Ben McCabe and Jeff Banner on Wanted bills. Does this mean anything to you?'

'No, it doesn't, Doc — except it doesn't make sense. You said I was missing. Where was I supposed to have gone? I must have told somebody. If I was a good company man I wouldn't have just lit out without saying anything. I would have told *somebody*.'

'But who, Ben? Who would you have told?'

'If Dredge wasn't around, there's only one other person in town who would have needed to know: the sheriff.'

Not for the first time, Nicholls and

Riley looked at each other.

At the time of the robbery and murder, Ned Miller was the sheriff of Charlsburg. He would have known.

7

Emily Troon sobbed herself to sleep many times during her painful, loveless marriage to the Reverend Tobias Troon. From the early days and the times when she had happily huddled in her man's arms as he stroked her hair after their love-making she had sensed that her husband's values were different from her own. But even when he brusquely ordered her out of his bed and to her own room, she put it down to his strict, disciplined ways. She did not doubt that he was a man full of devotion to his wife and to the ministry . . . a man of kindness and decency, loved by his small congregation at the tiny border township.

But time had changed the once devout man of the church into a zealot. Troon had always been a strong-willed, forceful character whose powerful voice and handsome features appealed to the female members of any church where he came to preach the Gospel.

Soon the numbers in the congregation far exceeded the number of seats in the pews as increasing numbers of parishioners flocked in eager to hear the man from Kansas. Troon quickly became aware that his popularity was not altogether due to his moving delivery of the readings from the Bible.

Emily first saw the change in her husband after an Easter service.

The church had been crowded, many of the townspeople paying their first visit since the arrival of Reverend Troon and his fire-and-brimstone sermon had won over a growing flock of listeners.

Especially among the women.

When the time came for the churchgoers to return to their homes and Emily sat waiting in the buggy to drive her husband to their little house on the edge of town, she was approached by a young member of the church — a boy whose mother she knew only vaguely

— delivering a message.

'The reverend said you were to go home, ma'am. He'll be along later.'

Emily thought little of it until her husband arrived almost four hours later. When she casually questioned him about the delay, he snapped back at her, 'Are you questioning me when I am on church business, woman? How dare you?'

'Tobias, I only — '

Before she could say another word, she was silenced by a glare of hostility and rage that she had never seen before. She turned and left the room. That night she was banished to her room and any effort at reconciliation was greeted with a sneering dismissal.

Within weeks the violence started. And the drinking. Until, at last, she could stand it no longer.

The neighbours talked behind her back; to her face they remarked on how ill she looked and asked markedly after her health. They knew what she had long guessed, that the town's great evangelist was involved with one or more of his congregation. That he drank heavily. But, despite everything his charismatic preaching continued to fill the pews of the small white church.

There were nights — a blessed relief from the humiliation — when Tobias Troon did not come home at all and, when he eventually rolled in after dawn, he was too drunk or too tired to do anything other than fall into his bed.

It was after one such night of neglect that Emily knew that she had to seek help to get her away from her prison. There was only one person to whom she could turn and she knew would come unquestioningly to her aid.

It was while Troon was out on one of his house visits that she slipped into town with her letter for the stage driver. She went home and prayed that her saviour would come soon.

But the weeks passed; the violence continued and there was still no sign of the brother to whom she had sent her letter pleading for him to take her away from her own private hell. Twice she tried to flee the marital home but each time Troon had foiled her attempt, which only earned her more punishment.

'You will obey me!' he yelled, his voice reaching screaming pitch and thrashing her with the strip of leather he kept by his bedside. 'God will be your judge! You will learn discipline.'

And so it went on until the night came when Emily Troon could stand it no longer. She sat cowering in the corner of her room, a shotgun on her knees as she waited for the man she hated most in the world to come home.

And all the time she prayed she would not be driven to killing. She prayed that the first man to walk through that door would be her brother, Ben McCabe.

*   *   *

Although he could remember so little of his life as a railroad agent, or where he had been on the night of the robbery, McCabe was now convinced that he was innocent of the crimes of which he was accused. He was no thief — and he was no killer. And there were others who believed in him: the doc, Sheriff Nicholls and, he hoped, the woman he had left behind at the farm, Beth. Then, as he stepped out into the sunlight, came another face from the past — a face that was to bring him back his memory, his sanity, and the will to hunt down the man who had wanted him killed.

And the hope that he was not too late to rescue a sister in distress.

8

Agnes Fraser had left Edinburgh with her husband on a great adventure to the new world, leaving behind the tenement buildings of Scotland's historic capital for the great outdoors of America's West.

'Schoolmasters will always be needed in the expanding towns and I will be among the leaders in my field,' her headmaster husband had informed her as they stood on deck and watched the coast slowly fade over the horizon. Before them, a new world, a new life in a young vibrant country.

'Loud and brash' he had described the Americans and brash they were to the unworldly Agnes, former seamstress and governess to the children of the influential Wallace family of industrialists in one of the wealthier suburbs of the great Scottish city.

She would have been happy to remain there, but the attraction of a new life for her husband had rubbed off on the pretty young wife and together they had made their plans, building their hopes around stories of small communities and the need for school-masters in the State of California. But fate conspired against the Frasers. James had never been the strongest of men, surrendering regularly to the ills that befell so many people who lived in the damp and cold environments of industrial Scotland.

Little more than a year after their arduous sea voyage and long before the Frasers reached the home of their dreams in California, James was taken by a fever. For many months Agnes nursed her sick husband, encouraged by occasional bouts of good health before he eventually succumbed on the eve of his fortieth birthday.

Distraught and alone, Agnes contemplated a return to her native Scotland, but chance played its hand to prevent her from taking that step. Her husband's funeral was attended by a governor of his school in Cheyenne, who was the owner of a boarding-house in the little town of Charlsburg. As fate would have it, the lady in charge of the lodging-house had been forced to resign her position to tend to her ailing mother and James Fraser's colleague wondered if the Scotsman's widow would be interested in taking up the position. The town would also provide extra income for her services as a seamstress or temporary schoolteacher.

With little money to replenish her savings, Agnes felt that a return to Scotland would be an admission of failure so she agreed to take over the running of the boarding-house.

From the first day she feared that the move had been a mistake. While some of her boarders were respectable travelling businessmen on a one or two night stopover on their journeys to the larger cities, many were loud and lewd cattlemen who abused her hospitality.

She was always happy to see the back of such patrons.

There was the occasional exception to both types — the long-term stayer who did not fit into either category. Not a suited businessman and certainly not an unprincipled cattle dealer.

One, especially, was a thoughtful, handsome man, only a few years older than herself who was far more than a paying guest. Several times he intervened in disputes with disagreeable boarders.

Three years had passed since James's untimely death and Agnes, still a young and pretty widow, had shunned the attentions of many an eager suitor, but she hoped the arrival of the tall stranger from Kansas might change all that. Instead, she soon discovered that the attraction was a one-way street and the new boarder was to treat her with the respect he offered all females.

In fact he was the perfect guest at her boarding-house until that fateful day . . . the day the letter arrived.

The delivery had been made shortly before noon but it was mid-afternoon by the time he returned to the house and she handed over the small package.

Within an hour and with hardly a word — other than a short explanation that he would be out of town for a few days on family business — he had packed a saddle-bag and ridden at high speed out of town.

That was the last Agnes Fraser had seen of her boarder until she stepped out of the general store and found herself gazing into the face of the man himself. More than a month after his departure her heart skipped a beat as she stared into the eyes of Ben McCabe.

★ ★ ★

He spoke first, a muttered apology for almost knocking her off her feet. Then, as though a light had been switched on in his head, came the realization that he knew the woman.

'Mrs Fraser! Agnes!'

Briefly stunned by the look of surprise on his face, she hardly knew how to reply. Regaining control she smiled up at him.

'I thought you had left town for good, Ben — er — Mr McCabe. I'm afraid I couldn't keep your room, but I put your things away in a safe place in case you decided to return, I — ' It seemed a feeble sort of reintroduction but she suddenly noticed his look of bewilderment. Concerned, she asked, 'Are you all right? You look, oh, I don't know . . . '

'No, no, I'm fine. It's just that for a moment there I thought I remembered something.'

Agnes relaxed.

'Remembered what?'

He didn't answer. At least not at first, not until he gathered his thoughts. Here he was facing a pretty young woman he knew from his recent past, the woman who ran the boarding-house where he had lived, the woman who had sparked a lost memory — a memory of a letter he had received from his sister pleading for help. He had taken a long hard ride out of Charlsburg, urged on by the contents of his sister's letter, but then what? Nothing. Until he woke up in a strange bed to be confronted by a Wanted poster bearing his name.

'Agnes, if you have a room, I will take it,' he said suddenly, an urgency in his voice. 'But I must warn you, my next exit from town may be even quicker than the last. I need to know what happened after I left town the last time.'

★ ★ ★

One month earlier . . .

Ben McCabe re-read the hurriedly scribbled letter. He hardly recognized the handwriting as that of his younger sister.

It was only the second time he had heard from her since her marriage to that preacherman whom he had disliked at first sight. But Emily had insisted that she loved him and who was he to argue with a strong-willed female? But now, as he folded the letter and returned it to its envelope there was proof that he had been right all along: the man was a bully, a brutal, wife-beating drinker whose Bible-thumping and God-bothering sermons were all the rantings of a man living a lie.

McCabe knew that time was short. His sister's letter would have been written two or three weeks earlier, so by now the whole situation may have changed for the worse.

Throwing the letter into a table drawer, McCabe crammed shirts and pants into saddle-bags and hurried down the stairs, passing a startled Agnes Fraser on the way.

'Sorry to rush off like this, Mrs Fraser. Got some family business to attend to and I may be gone a few days.'

With that he hurried past the startled Scotswoman and down the street to the livery where his horse must have been expecting another day of rest. Instead, Ben ordered the young ostler to saddle up then rode off at high speed.

Other pairs of eyes took a special interest in Ben McCabe's hurried departure from Charlsburg. Bewildered, Agnes Fraser stood on her porch as her gentleman boarder's horse kicked up the main street dust.

And leaning against the post outside the sheriff's office was crooked lawman Ned Miller. His eyes never left the clouds of dust until the rider disappeared behind the last building on the street. Then he turned to the sallow youth lounging on a wooden chair on the boardwalk.

'Now, where's he going in such an all-fired hurry?' he asked without expecting an answer. None came and Miller turned on his heel and headed for the railroad office. He was closely followed by Frank Beckman.

Three blocks away was an empty rail-office safe and the lifeless body of an old man. And a rider leaving town in a hurry. Ben McCabe was about to become a fugitive and he didn't know it.

Four days into his week-long ride to rescue his sister from a brutal husband Ben McCabe was gunned down and left for dead.

9

Agnes Fraser poured more coffee into her favourite china cup and passed it to McCabe who sat opposite her at the neatly arranged table in the boarding-house dining-room.

He had re-read the letter that had sent him on his mission of mercy and wondered whether it was too late to finish the rescue act — over a month since it first arrived.

Dearest Brother Ben

You will be surprised to hear from your sister after such a time but I am writing in the hope — no, praying — that you can help me. Life with Tobias is intolerable and I am very frightened. It is as you suggested. He has turned from a loving, caring husband into a violent brute and, I suspect, a philanderer. He still holds a position of prominence here in Ganson and his Sunday services are as well attended as ever, but his theatrical preachings are a long way different from the way we live our lives.

I hate to burden you with this, dear brother, but I do not know how much longer I can stand the humiliation, the beatings. I cry myself to sleep most nights and although I pray to God that one day some jealous husband will find him in a shameful situation and take instant and final reprisal, I fear that my God is not as heedful as Tobias's.

Some days, especially in full view of his parishioners, he is the perfect gentleman and the ladies of the town will hear no ill of him.

But believe me, brother, they do not know him. He is wicked and cruel and unless I flee from him, the day may soon come when I — or he — may be dead.

Please, please come as soon as you

can. I only hope that this letter is not too late.

Your loving sister, Emily

'You found this letter in my room and kept it for me? And you did not read it?' Ben said laying the paper aside.

Agnes gave him a look that suggested the idea never entered her head. 'I do not read other people's correspondence,' she said, the vexation in her voice bringing out the marked accent of the land of her birth.

Ben smiled. 'No, sorry I asked, but I have been away for some time — '

'One month less a few days,' she prompted him.

'And I never did get to see my sister,' he said sadly. 'And now it may be too late.'

'And perhaps it may not,' she said sharply. Again the accent was marked. 'You have other troubles, but your sister needs you. Everything else can wait, especially revenge on the people who have wronged you.'

He finished the last of his coffee and rose from the table.

'One more night will not make a difference. Early tomorrow I will be refreshed enough to finish the job I don't believe I even started. As you said, Mrs Fraser, the others can wait.'

'Agnes, please call me, Agnes,' she said, but she was not sure he heard as he climbed the stairs to his room for a night's sleep.

His mind was in turmoil as he lay staring up at the ceiling. Talking to Agnes Fraser had helped him to fill in many of the gaps in his memory. He could even picture his sister's face and that of the man she had married. Time was healing and although there were still blanks he eventually fell into a dreamless sleep . . .

★   ★   ★

While McCabe and Agnes Fraser talked over the reasons for his rapid departure from Charlsburg almost a month ago,

115

Mitchell Dredge sat alone in a bar in Laramie trying to think about his next move. Until he had walked in on the secretive conversation between Carla and Jay Munroe his plan had been close to perfect. McCabe had been the ideal scapegoat for the robbery and murder at the railroad office. His decision to put up a reward and issue Wanted posters on behalf of the company added to the growing belief in the region that the railroad's top detective had gone bad. It was not a view he intended to discourage. Indeed, he had actually sent Munroe in hot pursuit and hinted to Miller and that young hothead Beckman that there could be an additional $2,000 at stake if they carried out the job. It would do no harm to call on a few extra guns.

The killing of the old man had been unfortunate; probably Beckman's doing he thought, but that made the hunt for McCabe all the more crucial. The more guns the better.

He had wanted McCabe dead — not

brought back to face a trial. But McCabe was back. Munroe had failed him and now he was with Carla. Miller and the crazy kid had also failed.

On top of that, in a last desperate step to make up for the money he would be losing from any private dealings over cattle transport fees, he had emptied the company safe for a second time.

As he toyed with his glass he wondered why McCabe had failed to acknowledge him when they came face to face and the only solution he could reach was that, for some reason he did not understand, McCabe had simply failed to recognize him.

Jay had said he had put two bullets in the man and one, he swore had been to the head. Clearly it had not killed him, but it could have done other damage. Dredge was no expert in medical matters but he had heard stories of prizefighters taking so much punishment to the brain that they would not have known their own mother if they had bumped into her.

Could Jay's bullets have done the same to McCabe? And, if so, was the damage permanent? He couldn't take the risk, especially since he had learned that Carla and Jay were in cahoots and no doubt on his trail.

He had checked into the hotel and hurried up to his room. Once there he counted the money he had left from the robberies. A total of less than $20,000. Maybe enough for a small stake out West but well short of his dreams of a life of wealth and depravity. Filling his money belt with the notes, he stuffed the loot under the mattress and went down to the bar for a drink to relax his nerves.

He was still daydreaming about his Californian future when a shadow appeared over his shoulder. He turned to see a young, round-faced girl of no more than eighteen years smiling down at him.

''Scuse me, mister, did you drop this?' She had in her hand a small leather purse stamped with the monogram MED — Mitchell Edmund Dredge.

Dredge was instantly on his guard.

'Where d'you get this?'

The girl was unruffled. 'Why, I saw it on the floor just over there' — she pointed to a spot three feet from the table where he was sitting — 'and as it's such a pretty purse and we don't get too many real gentlemen in here, I just guessed — '

But Dredge wasn't listening. Instead he was examining the contents of the wallet. All the money, just over $100, was still there.

Only now did Dredge return the smile.

'I'm sorry, young lady, please, sit down. Join me in a drink to show my gratitude for your honesty. You look like the sort of young lady who would like champagne.'

Sarah Cotton held her smile. So easy, she thought, these pompous men in their smart suits who sat alone at the

119

tables, their heads turned by the slightest flattery. Their pockets were so easy to pick as they let their minds and eyes wander. But this one looked like extra easy pickings.

She could have kept the money and he would have been no wiser but she thought there might be much bigger rewards if she played it right. A glance at the barman and his returning nod was enough.

'What's your name, young lady?'

'I'm Dolly,' said Sarah still smiling, 'and you are — no, let me guess. M could be for ... Moses. No, I don't think so, how about Maximilian? No, you don't look like a Maximilian, my guess is it's Matthew — you're a Matthew. Am I right?' she giggled.

'Spot on, young lady — er, Dolly,' Dredge laughed, thinking, I'm no more a Matthew than you are a Dolly but let's play anyway.

The barman carried over a bottle of champagne with two glasses and laid them on the table. They sat staring at each other across the table as Dredge sipped his drink while the girl simply toyed with her glass. He gave himself another and when that was finished he moved to pour more drinks, not even noticing that her glass was still untouched.

He called for another bottle and when it arrived, Sarah rested her hand lightly but encouragingly on his arm.

Patiently, she waited while the man in the tight-fitting suit eagerly downed the champagne as though it was nothing more potent than a glass of lemonade. Satisfied that her latest victim was now well on his way to oblivion she leaned closer.

'Do you know, Matthew, maybe such a good wine should not be drunk in a bar room like this. It's more of a private enjoyment, don't you think? Maybe there's a room — '

Dredge looked at her eagerly. 'I have a room. It is very private — we could go there.'

Sarah linked her arm in his as he rose from the chair. 'Lead the way.' As they climbed the stairs, she glanced back at the barman, the signal that he was to come running if things went wrong. Not that she expected anything to go wrong. The drug was already in the bottle but she knew that it could take up to thirty minutes to take effect. Keeping this lustful man at arm's length for that long would not be a problem.

Once inside the room, Dredge placed the champagne and glasses on a bedside table and immediately started to unbutton his coat. Leering at the young woman in the off-shoulder dress and the winning smile, he moved towards her.

'Now, young lady, let's do the real business and forget all about twenty-dollar champagne, shall we?'

Sarah Cotton didn't flinch. It was exactly what she had expected and she was prepared for it. It happened every time.

'Why sure, Matthew, but maybe just one glass. After all, my boss would be not too pleased if I returned an unused bottle of his finest champagne.'

Dredge chuckled but it was an ugly snort of a sound without much humour. He knew that the bar owner didn't give a damn whether the wine was drunk or poured down the sink.

'Anything to please a pretty young thing like you,' he said, eagerly filling two glasses in his enthusiasm to pass through the preliminaries. He gulped the wine and his second glass went down just as quickly, even before 'Dolly' had raised her first to her lips.

Dredge studied the young girl opposite. Sure, she was a prostitute and a pretty one at that, but she was no Carla. Too young, for one thing. And too — what was it? He gulped down a third glass of the doctored champagne.

Sarah perched on the side of the bed. This was going even better than she had hoped.

The drug — a new thing with a funny name her disgraced doctor-turned-barman had told her — was supposed to take effect slowly but at the rate this man was gulping his wine he would soon be too drunk to get what he wanted anyway.

'Why — why won't you stand still, young lady, I-I — ' his voice became nothing more than a slur as he slumped back on to the bed.

Sarah 'Dolly' Cotton waited for several minutes to make sure that the drug had done its job and the man whose name she knew wasn't Matthew was asleep. She had already been told who he was — Mitchell Dredge, a leading railroad boss from Charlsburg.

Putting down her untouched glass and smiling at how gullible and unworldly men like this could be, Sarah immediately removed the sleeping man's wallet and extracted the wad from inside: $115. Then, spotting the carpetbag at the bedside, she tipped the contents out in search of any valuables and the money he was undoubtedly carrying.

A pocket watch fell to the floor, then a small, woman's pistol and a box of cigars. Frantically pulling at the clothes, Dolly found herself cursing aloud.

There must be more. No man wears such expensive suits, dressing like a dandy with only $115 to his name. She searched the drawers of the desk, then the cupboard in the corner.

She looked under the bed. Nothing. Not an extra dollar.

She stared down at the comatose figure on the bed. To her young eyes he was nothing more than a figure of fun, a man who presented himself as God's gift to womanhood but was a perfect specimen for scorn and ridicule. She was also angry enough to take a small measure of revenge for her meagre takings of $115.

Slapping the sleeping man's face to check that he was still comatose, she then set about undressing him and stuffing the clothes into the bag before hurling it out into the alley below.

She smiled at the thought of him waking naked, unable to remember how he got into such a state, or if he had enjoyed the experience. As a finishing touch she dropped his hat to cover his most private parts before leaving the room to go in search of her next, hopefully more rewarding, victim. At the foot of the stairs she encountered her barman partner who had supplied the drug and handed him his $50.

When Mitchell Dredge woke from his induced slumbers, naked and alone on a strange hotel bed, he panicked, frantically searching the room for his missing belongings. Slowly came the realization that he had been taken for a fool. Lifting the mattress he saw that the money belt was still there. The young, thieving bitch had missed that. And he could always buy some new clothes . . .

* * *

Ben McCabe was weary after his long ride from Charlsburg, in no state to challenge his sister's tormentor, or to rescue her from a marriage made in hell.

The long journey to Ganson, Colorado, had given him plenty of time to reflect on the events leading up to this day. It had been slow and painstaking but, thanks to the help of Agnes Fraser and his regular walks around the town, his memory was now almost fully restored. There were still some unexplained blank passages, but he suspected he might have to live with those, and he was able to remember most of what had occupied him up to receiving Emily's letter. Agnes Fraser's summary of what had happened in Charlsburg after he left, confirmed everything he needed to know.

After leaving his job as deputy to Ned Miller in Kansas, McCabe had joined the rail company on its security staff as a detective. At first the job was routine, mundane to the point of boredom as he checked loading and unloading, passenger safety and comfort. Then came the instruction to go to Cheyenne.

His superiors were suspicious that the local depot manager based at Charlsburg, a Mitchell Dredge, was not all he was supposed to be in the honesty stakes. He was, in the view of senior executives, taking more than his commission from the company.

It had taken McCabe only a week to confirm those feelings and, in addition, add further suspicion that the man could also have been involved as an insider in a series of robberies. His final report would mean a summons to the head office for Dredge.

It was while Dredge was 'away on company business' that McCabe received the letter from his distraught sister and had left the town in a hurry.

That night, the now disgraced sheriff Ned Miller and the absent Dredge — his alibi intact — carried out their plan to rob the railroad. That the poor old-timer cleaning up the place got in the way of a bullet was a stroke of bad luck, but it was balanced by the good luck of having McCabe ride out of town at just the right moment. The perfect suspect. Days later, Jay Munroe shot him and left him for dead.

McCabe clearly recalled the rest; Beth and her family caring for him; waking up to see a Wanted poster thrust in his face; the arrival of Miller and the younger man; the shoot-out that left Miller wounded and finally the return to Charlsburg.

Now, as he pulled up outside the small Colorado town of Ganson to settle down for the night, he hoped he was still in time for his sister. Tomorrow would bring the answer.

⋆　⋆　⋆

After a solid night's sleep, Ben woke to a sunny Sunday morning — one of many the area around the picturesque town of Ganson had enjoyed over the past few weeks. He had not been a regular worshipper since his school days back in Kansas where he and Emily went along to Sunday services with their parents who were friends of the local minister. It was a weekly ritual Ben became less inclined to pursue as he grew older and discovered that there was a world outside their small farm community.

He was still in his tender years when he learned to rope and brand a steer and, if the need ever arose — which it occasionally did after a night in town — to handle himself with his fists and a gun. Not that young Ben McCabe — still Benjamin to his parents — was a man of violence. His first two skirmishes came when he felt compelled to defend his sister from the unwanted attentions of a couple of drunken ranch hands, and he came off seriously worse in one of those two bouts of fisticuffs.

The McCabe family became innocent victims of one of the many feuds that lingered for years after the Civil War when their father was gunned down crossing the street. His killer was a long-time Confederate sympathizer who had been run to ground by a band of ex-Union men and had tried to shoot his way out of trouble. A stray bullet caught his father, Daniel McCabe, in the heart.

He died instantly and the family's life began to change forever.

Ben and Emily helped to comfort their mother through her grieving period and worked extra hours on the farm. But then the self-styled Reverend Tobias Troon came calling.

For some reason Ben was never able to understand, Emily was taken by the man who said he was merely calling as God's Messenger of sympathy for the widow and her two fatherless children.

The visits became more frequent and although Ben, now in his early twenties, had to admit that the reverend was a handsome enough fellow he couldn't shake off the bad feeling about him. Too much sincerity disturbed him. He knew that Troon wasn't right for his sister, although their mother, still a regular churchgoer despite her loss, appeared to take a liking to the visitor.

'You're too hard on the reverend, Benjamin,' she would say if he voiced any criticism of the way Tobias treated Emily, who hardly noticed that her new suitor talked more about himself than any other subject under God's sun.

When the pair eventually became betrothed, Ben did his best to persuade Emily to wait, that there was no rush and she could be making a big mistake because her intended was not a man to be trusted despite his claims that he was on speaking terms with the Almighty.

But he had nothing in the way of proof and a hunch was no help. For his sister's sake he let the marriage go ahead without incident although there was one occasion where he had to call on all his self-control.

For the sake of Emily and their mother and the wedding guests, he held back from offering Tobias a piece of his mind. The man was holding court in his usual pompous arrogant way and totally ignoring his bride. For some inexplicable reason, friends and guests as well as family saw something in the bridegroom that Ben was clearly missing.

A year after the wedding their mother was taken ill and died suddenly. Tobias conducted the funeral and, although it contained extra helpings of his own brand of hell fire and damnation type of preaching, Emily's husband managed to capture the mood of the small congregation who gathered for the funeral of the well-loved lady.

Even Ben was mildly impressed and he told Emily so when they were alone after the burial.

'Maybe I misjudged him, Em,' he said, as they strolled away together from the graveside. 'That was a fine sermon he gave.'

His sister was quiet for a moment and then said softly, 'Yes, Tobias is very good at sermons.'

To Ben, that hardly sounded like a ringing endorsement from a wife for a husband and he waited for Emily to elaborate, but she remained silent for several minutes. He pressed her.

'You don't sound too happy. Don't tell me married life has worn you out already?' He tried to make it sound like a teasing playful comment but she was clearly not responsive.

She tried to dismiss the mood as a symptom of the day, her mother's funeral only a few years after the death of their father and now news that Tobias was planning to leave Kansas and head for Colorado where he said he could do far more of God's work, converting the heathen masses as he called them.

This was news to Ben who always imagined his little sister living within calling distance.

'When will you leave?' he asked.

'In another month, Tobias says. Once our affairs are finished here.'

'Affairs?'

'Tobias has a buyer for the farm. He wants to sell.'

Ben was stunned. They had never spoken about any sale. Even though

Ben was now a deputy sheriff and spent little time out at the homestead, he was still taken by surprise at the announcement. Officially, he had no say in what happened, he had transferred his interest in the farm as a token wedding present, but he had not expected Emily to sell up and leave at such short notice. He felt hurt that she had not even discussed it with him.

'Is that what you want, Emily?'

Again her reply did not come instantly.

'It's what Tobias wants,' she said at last, and there the subject closed.

The next time he heard from her they were settled in the small Colorado town of Ganson and he was still deputy to Sheriff Ned Miller and it was a job he was growing less fond of with each passing day.

Miller had his own ideas of law enforcement and was a hard-drinking man of few principles and even fewer morals so when the offer to join the railroad as a security agent came his way, Ben took the chance.

Emily's first letter had been short almost to the point of being formal and was mainly about Tobias and how his flock was growing almost daily; how he was becoming a leading figure in the community by advising the elders on many forms of civic matters and how, she had gathered, the ladies so admired him. The only reference to herself came at the end when she wrote of how she helped Tobias at the church and assisted at the schoolroom. All for no pay, of course. Tobias did not wish her to be a working wife when he could more than adequately provide.

But then came that second letter, the one that had eventually brought him to the town of Ganson. His own tribulations may mean that he was too late, but Ben McCabe decided that the best way to find out was to become a churchgoer again for a day.

Even with the news from his sister's letters, he was surprised at the number of people who flocked that Sunday morning to the little white, red-roofed building that stood at the end of Ganson's main street. Whole families of grandparents to grandchildren made their way to the church to be met by a tall, handsome man in the black garb of a minister. It was a man who, even from a distance, Ben recognized as his sister's husband.

Tobias Troon greeted his parishioners with enthusiasm. There was no sign of Emily. Ben decided to wait until the last of the stragglers had been welcomed into the church, but he noticed that Tobias spent more time with the women, especially the younger ones, than with the men or the children, but he put this conclusion down to his inbuilt suspicions of the man's character.

The street was empty when he approached the church and, once inside, slipped into one of the few vacant pews at the back and waited for the service to start.

After the usual preliminaries that he

remembered from childhood, the Reverend Tobias Troon mounted the steps to his pulpit. In Ben's eyes it was more like an actor coming on stage. He was, as McCabe well remembered, an impressive orator. Several times the congregation released a loud and approving 'Hallelujah' and he half expected them to break out into applause. It reminded him of one of his few visits to the theatre when a touring party of English thespians performed a play by William Shakespeare, *Henry V.*

He clearly remembered the scene in which the English were fighting the French at a place called Agincourt. Tobias sounded as though he was leading this congregation into battle. He was impressive.

Before the end of the service, Ben slipped out unnoticed and took his place in a sheltered area across the street and waited for the congregation to disperse, leaving Tobias alone on the steps of the church. He was about to move when the minister went back inside. Surprised, Ben decided to wait for his reappearance.

Troon had no sooner disappeared than a rig, driven by a pretty young redhead, turned down the street at the side of the church and drew to a halt. Moving slightly to his right, Ben could keep the rig and the driver in full view.

A couple of minutes passed before Tobias emerged from the church's side entrance and climbed aboard the rig. As he did so he put his arm around the woman's shoulder and pulled her close to him, kissing her full on the mouth. Even to Ben's untrained eye it was far more than a friendly peck from the local clergyman.

He waited for the rig to pull away and head out of town before racing to the livery where he had left his horse on arriving in town.

Hurriedly, he mounted up and headed off in the direction Tobias and the woman had taken. He had no idea of the house in which his sister lived and he had expected to confront Troon at the end of the service. But now it seemed that the reverend had other plans that did not include going home to his wife. Ben felt the anger rising as he kicked his horse into a gallop and headed out of town.

He caught sight of them after about three miles. Tobias was helping the woman down from the rig which was tied to a small bush alongside a picturesque creek.

The perfect meeting place for young lovers, Ben thought. Except that Tobias Troon was not a young lover — he was in his late thirties and, as he crouched behind a bush, Ben could see that the woman, although attractive, was much the same age. The redhead reached into the rear of the rig and withdrew a wicker basket while Tobias spread a large blanket on a flat piece of ground near the water's edge. The pair embraced and made a move to settle on the blanket.

Ben decided it was time to act. He stepped out from behind the cover of the bush and strode towards the couple.

'Mornin', Tobias! Lovely day for a picnic.'

Troon swung round startled, instantly recognizing the man standing a few feet away.

'Benjamin!'

In one word he managed to convey surprise and horror at the sight of the newcomer.

'Mornin' again, Tobias. And Miss — ' He let his voice fade waiting for his sister's husband to make the introductions. In the years since they had last met Tobias had clearly lost none of his ability to talk his way out of an awkward situation.

'Benjamin . . . this is Mrs Claremont.' He tried a half-hearted chuckle. 'Things are not what they appear. She was recently widowed and came to me for spiritual counselling. I am helping her to cope with her grief.'

'I can see that, Reverend,' Ben answered, his voice heavy with sarcasm. 'And where's Emily?'

Tobias Troon suddenly had the look of a man close to panic.

'Emily?'

'Your wife, Mr Troon. My sister. I'm here to visit her.'

Then, with a theatrical gesture, the clergyman regained his composure.

'Visit her?'

'Then if what she tells me is true, I'll be taking her away from here.'

'Take her away? But that won't be possible. Not possible at all. I'm afraid the Good Lord in His wisdom has called first.'

His reply, delivered with all the bluster and pomposity, stunned Ben, taking him completely off guard.

'She's — she's dead?' he stammered.

Tobias Troon was back in control of the situation. He turned to the woman. 'I must ask you should leave us alone for a moment, my dear. Mr McCabe and I have matters to discuss.'

As the woman walked away towards the rig, Troon said quietly, 'I'm sorry if I shocked you, Benjamin. No, Emily is still with us but not for much longer I fear. If God is merciful, she will soon be at peace.'

He moved to put his arm around Ben's shoulder but McCabe backed away.

'What's going on? Where is she? Are you telling me she's dying? What's wrong with her?' The rapid fire questions failed to rattle Troon who, fully recovered from the initial shock of seeing Ben standing over him, chose his next words carefully.

'I'm truly sorry to be the bearer of bad news but all the doctors who have seen poor Emily have told me that the sickness is terminal and that she has little more than a few days. I'm deeply sorry.'

'So you said,' Ben snapped back. 'Where is she? I want to see her.'

'She needs to rest so, I'm sorry, I can't allow that,' Tobias said softly but was shocked when Ben turned and glared at him.

'I'm not asking you, Troon. You're

through giving orders to me. Now — where is she?'

The threat in Ben's voice took Tobias by surprise. He thought he had won over his unwelcome relative but it was now clear that he had not.

'Please, Benjamin, for Emily's sake, she wouldn't want you to see her as she is. She would want you to remember her as she was.'

Ben dismissed that idea at once. He didn't trust Troon and if Emily was in such a bad state she would need all the help she could get. Her husband, too busy giving 'spiritual guidance to a grieving widow' clearly hadn't time to do his duty.

'Go to hell, Troon,' he barked and then, without another word, Ben brushed past the clergyman and headed for his horse. If the minister wouldn't help him, he would find his own way to the church house. Somebody in town would tell him. He had to see his sister. He had to learn the truth about her sickness.

Tobias Troon watched him go. The Claremont 'widow' had returned from the rig and was linking her arm through his. She gazed up into his eyes and smiled.

'Perhaps it is best this way, Tobias. Once he knows how ill she is, he will understand why we are together like this.'

Troon did not return the smile. He knew that, whatever the future had in store for him, it was certainly not for the best.

★ ★ ★

The streets of Ganson were deserted when Ben rode back into town. It was a few minutes after noon when he pulled up outside the sheriff's office, tied his horse to the hitching rail and mounted the boardwalk.

The door was locked and looking through the window he could see that the office was deserted. In Ganson it appeared that even the law took time off to listen to the Reverend Tobias Troon's sermons.

Fortunately, for Ben, the town's bar owners had no such delusions of godliness and the saloon across the main street was open for business.

As Ben pushed his way through the batwings the barman paused from his job of polishing the counter and looked up. At a table across the room four men were playing cards. One of them was wearing a star — so much for Ben's initial assumption of the local sheriff's moral standing. His absence from office had far more to do with a card table than the pulpit.

'Afternoon, stranger. What can I get you?' The barman offered a cheerful friendly smile of welcome as Ben wandered over to the bar.

'I'll take a beer — and some information,' he said, throwing a couple of coins on to the bar top.

'I can let you have the beer, mister — ain't too sure about the information, though.'

'It's no big secret,' Ben said pleasantly. 'Just want you to point me the way to the minister's house.'

The barman finished pouring the beer. 'You'll find it just past the church, an old blue place. Looks a bit rundown for a clergyman's house. Don't reckon you'll find Tobias there, though, if that's who you're lookin' for. He don't spend too much time there, these days, not since what happened to his wife'n all.'

Ben sipped his drink.

'What happened to her?'

'We-ell, don't rightly know. Lovely lady, Mrs Troon. Seems she took ill all of a sudden and was taken away. Here one day and gone the next. The reverend said they had taken her to a sanitorium back East but nobody seen her go.

'We was all surprised when he didn't go with her, but he said he had to stay and do God's work and that his wife understood.' He paused briefly and then leaned across, beckoning Ben closer.

'I ain't no churchgoer, mister, so I don't need to listen to what Tobias preaches, but if you ask me, he wasn't too sorry to see his wife taken away. Ever since she's gone he's been keeping close company with Dan Claremont's widow. Spiritual counselling, he calls it. Dan's been dead more 'n a year now, so I reckon the counselling our reverend's givin' her ain't got nothing to do with churching, if you get my meaning.'

Ben finished his beer in a hurry and muttered his thanks to the bartender before heading out into the hot sun.

The street was still quiet and on many another day he would have taken an instant liking to the town. But today he was in no mood to admire the niceties of neatly arranged flower gardens, picturesque houses and a backdrop of tall trees and distant hillsides.

He was too late. Emily had gone to a sanitorium. Back East, the barman said. Back East and alone while her treacherous husband carried out his godly duties by keeping company with another woman.

Ben felt his anger rising, as much with himself for his failure to rescue Emily as with the man he felt was responsible for her unhappiness and sickness. He felt so helpless — his dying sister was lying in some far-off hospital bed and he could do nothing.

As he stood and stared out at the smart main street, he thought about his return to Charlsburg to pick up the rest of his life and, if he still felt so inclined, go after the man who had put his face on Wanted posters for a crime he did not commit; the man he knew was truly responsible for the robbery and murder for which he had been hunted — Mitchell Dredge.

Deep in thought and thoroughly dejected, he trudged slowly across the street, head bowed, to where he had hitched his horse. He failed to notice Tobias's rig as it turned into the street behind the church.

Suddenly McCabe came to a decision that he knew that he should have made instantly. He would get Troon to tell him where Emily was and, whatever her faithless husband's twisted opinion, he would go to her. Somebody had to be at her bedside at the end and, if Troon wasn't going to be there, it was up to Ben to see that she did not die alone. Following the directions given to him by the bartender, Ben strode purposefully along the street to prepare for Troon's return, but he was surprised to see that the rig was already there although there was no sign of the man himself.

His first knock on the door brought no response so he tried again, harder than before.

This time Tobias opened the door and stepped into the open. He was pointing a derringer at McCabe's chest.

Ben edged away, raising his hands in mock surrender.

'Steady, Tobias, there's no call for a gun. I only want to talk.'

But there was fire in Troon's eyes. A face full of hate was glaring at McCabe.

'I told you!' he snarled. 'You're not wanted here. Get out ... get out before ... ' He waved the small gun threateningly. 'Just leave us alone!'

'Right,' said Ben soothingly. 'Just tell me — '

Before he could finish the sentence he heard the noise. A muffled cry that came from inside the house behind Troon. Ben rushed forward, catching the startled clergyman offguard. Knocking him aside and sending the gun spinning from his grasp, Ben gripped the door handle, but before he could enter the house, Troon was back on his feet.

Screaming foul abuse, he tried to grab McCabe's arm but Ben spun round, catching the other man full in the face with his elbow.

There was another cry from inside the house and this time there was no mistaking the voice: it was Emily!

Putting his shoulder to the door, Ben burst into the house. The room was empty but in the far corner was another door and the cries were coming from the other side. Looking round, he saw that Troon was scampering towards the derringer lying on the porch. Although desperate to get to his sister, McCabe knew that he could not let Troon reach the weapon and the hesitation was almost fatal.

Troon was stretching for the gun when Ben leapt at him. The two men rolled out into the street and grappled in the dust.

Ben was surprised at the strength of the other man as the two struggled to their feet.

A wildly swung punch glanced McCabe's temple but in return, he smashed his fist into the jaw of the minister who staggered backwards but managed to keep his feet.

Roaring like a man demented, he launched himself at McCabe, throwing his arms around the younger man's waist to send him crashing to the dust. The pair traded blows and McCabe felt the taste of blood as a fist caught him full on the jaw.

Troon may have been a bully but he was not the kind who backed away when confronted by somebody who would fight back. Struggling to his feet, Tobias reached for a loose stone which he hurled at McCabe. Luckily, it went over his shoulder and smashed the house window.

Ben ducked to avoid another swinging blow delivered with such force that it was enough to send Tobias spinning off his feet and crashing into the porch. Blind rage was spurring him on, but, as he rose to his feet, he was met by a fierce right from McCabe that sent him crashing through the surround, splintering the wood and scattering the fragments into the street.

Tobias lay still.

Ben hurried inside the house, dashed across the room and pulled open the door. Behind it the room was in semi-darkness, but there was no mistaking the figure cowering in the corner, sobbing hysterically. Ben knelt down and put his arms comfortingly around his sister.

153

'Don't worry, Emily, it's over. He'll never touch you again.'

'Who's that?' She looked up through bruised bewildered eyes. 'Who's there?'

As his eyes became accustomed to the dim light in the shuttered room he could see that his sister was a forlorn shrunken figure clad in torn, stained clothes no better than rags.

'In God's name, what's been happening?' he whispered, as he eyed the scene. Carefully he lifted the lightweight woman and rested her on the crumpled bed that was no larger than a prison bunk.

Hurriedly searching through drawers and the one cupboard in the corner, he bundled clothes into a battered bag and left the room. Outside the ruckus had caught the attention of a few neigbours and a small crowd had gathered.

Two women were comforting Troon. He had regained consciousness and was sitting on the porch steps. McCabe stepped through them, threw the clothes bag into the rig and returned to the house.

As he passed, one of the woman who had been trying to comfort Tobias rose to her feet and confronted him.

'What's happening here, mister?' she asked, her voice full of aggression. 'What've you done to the reverend?'

Ben looked down in contempt at the stricken clergyman.

'Ask him!' he spat. 'Or, better still — ' He grabbed her arm and, despite her protests, dragged her into the house. Pushing her across the room he snapped: 'In there — go and see what your precious minister has done to his wife.'

The woman hesitated and then, seeing the anger in the stranger's eyes, turned and entered the darkened bedroom.

Ben waited until the woman reappeared, a look of horror on her ashen face.

'That was done in the name of God!' Ben told her. 'Now I want you to go out there and tell your neighbours that this town is looking for a new minister. I'm sending the one you've got now straight to Hell.'

McCabe was reaching for his gun when he heard the voice, feeble as it was, coming from its frail broken body.

'No, please — no.'

He turned to see Emily clutching at the doorpost.

The Ganson woman hurried over to support her. 'We should call the sheriff. And a doctor. She needs a doctor.'

'No. Not the sheriff,' Emily protested feebly, slumping to her knees. 'No — no sheriff.'

'That's right, my dear — we don't need the sheriff, do we?'

Ben spun round to see the figure of Tobias filling the doorway.

'He wouldn't understand. About discipline. All sinners need discipline. The Good Book tells us of Sodom and Gomorrah. Of Lot's wife being turned to a pillar of salt because she looked back; of vengeance — '

He was ranting, his voice raising from a barely audible whisper into a manic roar. It was as though he was in his pulpit, spitting fire and brimstone, condemning sinners to Hell's eternal flames and damnation. Then, just as suddenly it left him to be replaced by cold-eyed reason.

'I told you, McCabe,' he said quietly. 'You are not wanted here. Emily does not need you. She wants you to leave.'

Ben made a move towards him but froze at the sight of the small handgun pointed at his chest. He had retrieved the derringer.

'Reverend!'

The Ganson woman almost screamed the word and it was enough to catch Troon off guard.

Ben reached for his six-gun and threw himself to the floor as he did so. Tobias fired but it was an aimless shot, the bullet flying harmlessly wide of its target and smashing into the wall behind McCabe.

The talking was indeed over. Ben

squeezed the trigger of his Colt and, unlike Tobias, his aim was true. The man in the black garb of a churchman clutched his chest, his eyes agape at the realization that he had been hit. There was death on his face as he slumped to his knees before collapsing fully stretched face down.

The Ganson woman screamed.

Ben rose slowly to his feet, holstered his six-gun and turned to where Emily clung on to the doorpost for support. She was still sobbing. He wrapped a shawl around her shoulders and led her from the house. Neighbours were gathering around the body of their preacher. Tobias Troon had given his last sermon.

Silently, Ben settled Emily on to the rig and climbed up beside her.

The good people of Ganson would have to explain to their sheriff what had happened to their minister. Ben had more things to worry about than the death of a man who was closer to the Devil than the God he claimed to represent.

The journey back to Charlsburg would be long and painful and he did not know whether his newly-widowed sister had the will power to survive.

⋆   ⋆   ⋆

By the third day of their long trek, Emily had in fact recovered enough in mind and body to relate to Ben the details of her horrendous marriage to a minister who became a brutal tyrant.

It all started when the money from the sale of the family farm began to run out and Tobias's powers of persuasion failed to impress the group of gamblers with whom he had become increasingly involved. He began to stay away from the house and, when he did return, he was full of hate and anger, followed regularly by what he described as 'God's punishment'.

Emily, once a stalwart of the church, became a prisoner in her own home — a slave to her husband's power and vanity.

She had already heard stories, including the mysterious and unsolved killing of rich cattleman Dan Claremont, dragged from his bed in the middle of the night and gunned down in a back alley.

Tobias had rushed to the widow's side offering, he claimed, comfort and understanding to the poor woman. By then Emily knew that such qualities were no longer part of her husband's character.

And there were others, wealthy widows all, who were 'comforted' by their preacher.

The beatings became more frequent and when Ben did not reply to her letter pleading for help, Emily was in deep despair.

Tobias told inquisitive neighbours that his wife was too ill to see visitors until, eventually, he said she had had to be moved to a sanitorium in the middle of the night.

Ben listened to his sister's confused account of her living hell with a growing feeling of despair at his failure to answer her call. His own problems — clearing his own name and bringing others to justice — could wait.

'Tobias is dead. He can't hurt you any more,' was all he could offer and his sister raised a feeble smile.

'I know,' she said. 'Thank you.'

And at that she slid back into her own silent world, shutting out her brother and memories of her brutal husband.

10

Mitchell Dredge threw down his cards in disgust. His luck had been out ever since that thieving saloon slut had tried to separate him from his money.

At least she had failed and he still had that — or most of it. He had picked up too many losing hands since that night in Laramie.

What else could go wrong? he wondered, draining his whiskey glass and heading for the bar.

He had thought his plan was perfect, offering a $2,000 reward to the likes of Munroe, Miller and the kid Beckman. Printing Wanted posters added an extra touch of legality.

But the three of them had failed miserably — especially Munroe. Now not only was McCabe likely to be on his tail, but Carla was in cahoots with Munroe and he still had no notion of the whereabouts of Beckman and that crook of a sheriff, Miller.

'Whiskey,' he grunted at the barman, 'and leave the bottle.'

Alone, Dredge studied the occupants of the small, haze-filled room. A girl, not unlike the one who had tried to rob him back in Laramie, was singing at a piano but nobody was listening,

Two card games other than the one he had left were causing some heated discussion, as was the dice table. The rest of the customers were just drinkers. Dredge downed his whiskey and refilled his glass.

God! Have I been reduced to this? he thought self-pityingly. It was time to move on. California was still a distant dream but even so far away it was better than this one-horse town of deadbeats and old soldiers.

Dredge was much the worse for drink when he eventually staggered out of the small saloon to make his way to his rented room. He paid no attention to the two riders who were hitching their horses to a rail on the opposite side of the street.

But they noticed him before they entered the saloon: Munroe and Carla were in town.

★ ★ ★

Agnes Fraser turned away from the woman in the bed and left the room.

'She's had a bad time, Mr McCabe,' she said, her voice barely above a whisper as she closed the bedroom door quietly behind her. 'The doctor has ordered complete rest — and then some. She can stay here as long as it takes.'

Ben was grateful. Ever since she had finished telling him about her life with Tobias Troon, his sister had retreated into a shell, as though she wanted to raise a barrier between herself and the rest of the world.

'Can I leave her with you?' he asked hopefully.

Agnes smiled. 'I know you have things to do, people to find, even scores to settle and you won't rest easy until that's done,' she said.

It could have been a criticism but she made it sound like encouragement — as though she knew exactly what he had to do.

'It may take some time,' he said quietly. 'I'm not even sure I know where to start looking — or what I'll do when I get there.'

Again, Agnes offered an encouraging smile. What was it about this man that made her heart flutter unlike it had ever done before, even during the early days of her courtship with James?

Sure, he was tall and handsome, but she had seen and known plenty such men and they had not had this effect on her. Like she was a schoolgirl again. He had kind eyes, she could see that, and if his concern for his sister was any guide he had genuine feeling about other people. And his manners were impeccable. She chuckled as she reminded herself that she was making Ben McCabe sound too good to be true.

'Whatever it is, I'm sure you'll do the right thing . . . Ben. And don't worry about Emily, I'll take care of her.'

He leaned down and kissed her on the cheek.

'Thanks,' he said, 'maybe one day I can repay you.'

He turned and left the house before she could speak. Although he did not know where he was going to start his search for Mitchell Dredge he knew one man who might be able to help. His first stop would be the sheriff's office and a chat with Brad Nicholls.

★ ★ ★

Nicholls liked this man McCabe and he wanted to help. He listened in silence as his visitor outlined his plan to track down Mitchell Dredge and bring him back to Charlsburg to stand trial for robbery — and probably murder.

'It's a wide-open country out there, Brad, and I think I'm gonna need a bit of help.'

Nicholls gave him a puzzled look. 'What kinda help?'

'Like I said, it's a big country — maybe you might have some idea where I could start looking.'

Nicholls thought for a moment. Then he reached inside his desk drawer and pulled out a newspaper.

'Take a look at that,' he said, pointing to an article at the foot of the page. 'Mister Dredge has been drawing attention to himself. Even by Laramie standards a man running through the street in nothing more than a towel and a hat wouldn't go unnoticed. Seems he went chasing after some saloon girl who had thrown his clothes out of the window and into a back alley. Dredge's job as railroad manager meant he's even known in Laramie so the local paper carried the story.'

McCabe allowed himself a chuckle, more at the thought of Mitchell Dredge roaming semi-naked down a Laramie back alley than at any sense of humour in the newspaper article.

He tossed the paper back on to the desk.

'That's somewhere to start,' he said. 'Anything else that might help?'

Again Nicholls paused before answering. Then: 'This may not help at all, especially if our man is still of the same mind. That Laramie incident was over a week ago and the only place I ever heard Dredge talk about was California and how some day he'd get there. He's sure got a head start on you if that's where he's figuring on going.'

McCabe shrugged. 'Then I've got a lot of ground to make up. Best be going, though there's one more thing you can do, Sheriff: give me a badge. Make me a deputy.'

'Sure, I can do that,' Nicholls said, reaching into his desk drawer for a deputy's tin star. 'But it won't count for much — not once you leave the territory.'

'I know that, but Dredge won't. That's all I'll need.'

'Good luck, then,' Nicholls said, as

the two men shook hands.

'See you soon, Sheriff.'

'I hope so, Ben — but I don't reckon on it being soon.'

★ ★ ★

In the days that followed Ben McCabe had no idea that he was on the trail of a man under a death sentence. Mitchell Dredge was already living on borrowed time.

11

Mitchell Dredge moved the lace curtain to one side, just enough to give him a sight of the street below. It was dark and deserted but that did not make him feel any easier. The suspicion that he was being watched would not go away. Perhaps it was the feeling that haunted every man carrying the guilt of having $20,000 of stolen money tied around his middle.

Behind him, the latest addition to his list of female conquests breathed heavily in the midst of her deep sleep, satisfied, Dredge told himself, by their earlier contortions.

She had not been a Carla, of course, but then, no woman could follow her — cheating bitch though she had turned out to be. He removed a couple of bills from his roll and threw them on the pillow beside the woman's head.

She had been worth that, he reflected, but now was the time to move on, while the town slept.

California was still a long way off and there were many more small towns and their women to sample before he reached the West Coast. And his luck at the tables was sure to change soon.

Silently and swiftly he packed his bag, checked that he had not left anything other than the few dollars and a half-finished bottle of the hotel's cheapest champagne, and left the room, closing the door quietly behind him.

Downstairs the place was deserted and in darkness. He had stabled his rig at the livery near the far end of the street and even though he heard nothing and saw nothing as he made his way along the boardwalk he was on edge until he reached the yard. Once there, he hitched up the horse, loaded the rig and prepared to leave town.

It was then that he heard the noise. Was it the sound of a gate creaking in the breeze? There was no breeze; it was a still, silent night. It must have been his imagination. He stopped and listened. Nothing.

It *was* my imagination, he told himself. But then it came again, this time accompanied by a click. And it was not in his imagination.

'Runnin' out on us, Mitch?'

They stepped out of the darkness, side by side. Jay Munroe and Carla Blake. And Munroe was pointing a gun at Dredge's chest.

He started to sweat. He had been followed — all the way from Charlsburg.

'Running out?' There was panic in those two words.

The pair advanced from the shadows towards him.

'That's what I'd call it, Mitch.' Munroe was in control. 'Now, we don't have any problem with you moving on and leaving us here, 'cept for one thing.'

Dredge knew what was coming but he did not wait.

It was time to go on the attack.

'You already cheated me once, Jay.

You told me McCabe was dead, that you'd gunned him down. But he ain't, is he? He ain't dead and sooner or later he'll be coming after me. And you. And her.' He pointed at Carla whose sneering look had disappeared.

'What's he saying, Jay? Who's McCabe?'

'Hah! He hasn't told you, has he? Five thousand dollars to kill a man who robbed the railroad.' There was no point in telling her the truth at this stage; and five thousand sounded a hell of a lot better than two. 'And I paid him.'

'Shut up, Dredge!'

Munroe gripped the gun tighter and there was anger in his eyes.

'Get the bag!' He snapped an order and Dredge tensed as the woman edged slowly towards the rig. What would Munroe do when they found nothing? He would know that the railroad boss would not leave town without the money he had stolen from the office safe.

But, frightened though he was,

Dredge was not going to give it all up without a struggle. Physically, he was no match for Munroe, but he had to act fast. He waited until Carla stepped between him and Munroe and then made his move. Grabbing her by the arm, he dragged her in front of him and then, spinning her round to act as a shield, he withdrew his small handgun and pressed its short barrel against her throat.

Carla struggled but Dredge's grip was vice-like.

'Drop the gun, Jay,' he growled, with a calmness he wasn't feeling. 'Just drop it, or Carla here might just get hurt.'

Munroe didn't move. Instead he just offered a twisted grin.

'You never were much of a bluffer, Mitch. An' I'm calling yuh.'

'No, Jay, he means it. He'll shoot.'

But Carla's plea left Munroe unmoved.

'Then what will he do, Carla? Attack me with that toy pistol? I'll take my chances.'

His voice was a sneer that told Carla

174

her life meant nothing to him. And it told Dredge that, as a hostage, she was worthless.

'So, what's it gonna be, Mitch? You shoot her and I kill you and take the money, or you hand it over all peaceful like and Carla and me, we ride out of here, leaving you with your hide in one piece. It's your move.'

It was stalemate and Dredge could feel panic taking over.

Carla pleaded, 'Let me go, Mitch, please — he'll kill us both.'

Dredge knew that his next move could be vital — maybe even a matter of life or death. Bracing himself, he shoved the woman towards Munroe and dived for the cover of an empty stall and darkness. The small handgun was no match for Jay's Colt, but now was not the time to study the odds. It was all he had.

Munroe's first bullet was well off target, smashing into the fence high above Dredge's head. Scrambling frantically on all fours, he managed to reach the gate before Munroe fired again. This time the shot ripped through a saddle blanket draped inches from his shoulder.

There was a brief silence. Dredge wondered how long it would be before the gunshots attracted attention and some curious — probably drunken — bypasser looked in. Nobody came.

The seconds ticked by. Where was Munroe? And where was Carla? Dredge gripped the small gun tightly. He knew that his only hope of getting out alive was to make a dash for it and use the dark back alleys behind the main street as cover. But how long could he run and hide? And how long would it be before Munroe realized that the money was not in the valise or the rig, but was strapped around Dredge's stomach? On an impulse, Dredge launched himself towards the stable door, banging his leg on a broken stake. He stifled a yell of pain, but the movement alerted Munroe. Another gunshot — and this time the bullet found its target, burying itself deep in Dredge's shoulder.

He screamed. In an instant Munroe was standing over him, his six-gun aimed at the wounded man's chest. Even in the darkness, Dredge could make out the crooked grin that he had come to hate so much. And to think that this was a man he had trusted. Beside him, Carla looked down on him in pity.

Gasping for breath, Dredge groaned his feeble surrender.

'All right, Jay, you win. The money's here in my belt.' He pointed towards his stomach. 'Take it. Take it all. Just get me a doctor. I'm hurt . . . I need a doctor.'

Munroe knelt down, took a cursory look at the damage his bullet had done, then ripped open Dredge's shirt. The humourless grin never left his face.

'You know, Mitch,' he said icily, 'it wasn't nice of you runnin' out on me and Carla after what I'd done for you.' Roughly, he removed the belt from around the injured man's waist. 'An' what have we got? Twenty? Twenty-five thousand dollars?'

'Please, Jay, I'm begging you — take the money, but get me a doctor. I'm hurtin' real bad.'

'Sure, Mitch, but you know something else, old friend,' he said, rising to his feet and throwing the money-belt over his shoulder. 'You don't need a doctor' — he aimed his gun at Dredge's head and squeezed the trigger — 'you need an undertaker.'

* * *

Carla thought she had seen all the worst in men, from life under her brutal, drunken father and a violent — now thankfully dead — husband, through all those she had met and bedded as a saloon singer. She had never met any man who could inspire love or loyalty. But she had lived a hard life and she had taken the regular knocks it had thrown at her in her stride and she had come through it almost unscathed. Until now.

As she stared into the face of Jay Munroe, his ice-cold blue eyes, his twisted grin, she saw something she had never seen in any man before — a face full of hate and blood lust. For the first time in her life, Carla Blake was truly afraid.

12

Ben McCabe looked down at the white lifeless, face in the open coffin. 'That's our man,' he said quietly. 'That's Dredge.'

McCabe had returned to his job with the railroad company and was in the office when the telegraph arrived reporting that a man carrying identification papers of the company's district manager had been found shot dead in a stable yard outside of Laramie and would somebody like to identify the body before the burial?

The sheriff nodded to the undertaker to close the lid and turned to McCabe.

'Sorry I had to get you out for this,' he muttered, but was surprised to see a smile appear on his visitor's face.

'Sorry? Don't be sorry, Sheriff. From what I've found out in the last few days, the man in that box put a price on my head and wanted me dead. He also robbed the railroad of thousands of dollars, so save your sympathy for some other poor soul.'

The local lawman nodded. 'Don't expect we'll ever find who did this.'

The two men walked out into the sunshine, leaving the undertaker to finish off before the burial.

'Whoever did it will be long gone by now,' the sheriff added, as the pair stepped out into the street.

'And with twenty thousand dollars in his saddle-bag,' McCabe suggested.

'You think they got all his money?' the sheriff asked.

'I don't think he was killed for the hell of it, though the shooter sure enjoyed what he was doing. A bullet in the shoulder and another in the head just to make sure he didn't talk. I wonder, maybe . . . ' McCabe paused, deep in thought. Did Dredge know his killer? It seemed likely. This was no chance shooting. Dredge had been carrying $20,000. Somebody must have known, and unless McCabe was badly off target, that somebody would have known all about Dredge. Which, if he figured right, included just about everybody in Charlsburg.

McCabe nodded a friendly farewell to the sheriff and crossed the street to where he had hitched his horse. It was a long ride back to town and he had a lot of thinking to do. The death of Dredge meant that the man who had set him up for robbery and murder was no longer on his wanted list. But he knew that the rotund railroad manager had not been the man who had put a bullet in him and sent him into the coma that almost cost him his memory. That would-be killer was still at large — and McCabe was determined to bring him to justice.

* * *

Carla sat in silence as she rode alongside Jay Munroe back along the trail to Charlsburg. The cold-blooded murder of Mitchell Dredge was still on her mind and the look on Munroe's face as he squeezed the trigger to end the railroad man's life would haunt her for a long time.

The horror of seeing the heartless and needless killing had left her stunned while Munroe coolly dragged the lifeless body deep into the darkest corner of the stable yard. Then, throwing the money belt over his left shoulder, he had grabbed Carla's arm, grinned and together they left the murder scene and headed for the saloon.

Munroe had muscled in on a poker game, drunk himself into a state of insensibility and finally been dragged away by a worried Carla to a room to sleep it off.

It was while Munroe was deep in his stupor that she came to her decision. She had to get away from him; away from the grip of fear in which she felt she was being held. The thrilling sense of risk, the idea of flirting with danger that had got into her when she had first succumbed to Jay's charms were things of the past.

Jay Munroe was evil.

The chance to make her escape under the cover of darkness was tempting. While Munroe slept off his drinking session she could be well clear of town, heading back into Laramie and maybe beyond. But she dismissed that idea almost immediately. He would come after her, furious that she had walked out on him, and an angry Munroe was a dangerous killer, as she had already witnessed.

Carla spent the rest of the night in an armchair planning her future. Munroe walking free would always be a threat but she could hardly walk into the nearest sheriff's office and tell the law what she knew without implicating herself in the murder and the robbery.

She had to find another way to rid herself of Munroe and at the same time get her hands on the money.

By the time Munroe had recovered and the pair were making their silent journey along the road back to Charlsburg, Carla had made her plans. She would use the man Ben McCabe to get what she wanted.

13

There was sadness and a hint of sorrow in Agnes's Scottish lilt as she spoke softly to Ben McCabe.

'She has been like that ever since you left,' she said, her voice scarcely above a whisper. 'Just sitting there and staring out of the window. She says nothing; eats very little. I don't know what to do.'

Ben had returned to the boarding-house to find that his sister failed to acknowledge him; it was as though he was a total stranger.

'What does the doctor say?' he asked.

Agnes sighed. 'You know Doc Riley. I'm afraid he is more used to dealing with bullet wounds and broken limbs than anything to do with the workings of the mind. He knows that there are more ways to damage a person than with physical violence, but he's at a loss

186

to know how to deal with it.'

Ben could see the distress in his sister's face as she sat staring aimlessly at nothing in particular. At that moment he felt that if he could have killed Tobias Troon a second time he would have happily done it. It was little comfort to know that his sister's evil husband was already rotting in Hell.

'What can we do? What can anybody do?' he said, a feeling of hopelessness in his gesture.

'She needs help from people who know about such things.' There was a long pause before Agnes said, 'Ben, we have to get Emily to go back East. Chicago, maybe, some big city to get that help.'

Agnes studied the man who had reached into her heart and she could see in his eyes a look of despair; a man who felt helpless in the face of a problem he did not understand.

'Don't worry, Ben.' She rested her hand lightly on his arm. 'We'll find a way to help your sister. I'll go with her

— together we'll get her through this.'

On an impulse Ben wrapped his arms around Agnes and pulled her close to him.

'Thanks, Agnes,' he whispered, suddenly feeling the urge to kiss her. She did not resist as he lifted her almost off her feet. Their embrace was long and warm before Agnes suddenly broke away, flustered and embarrassed. She moved to step away, but Ben grabbed her wrist and pulled her back.

'Thanks, Agnes,' he said again, before releasing her and leaving the house. She watched him go down the footpath and out into the street, heading towards town. As he disappeared from view she went back inside and wondered what the future had in store for them.

* * *

The lone gunman eyed his target, set himself, his feet shoulder-width apart. Carefully, he loosened the six-gun in its holster and practised his draw for the twentieth — or was it thirtieth — time that morning. Soon he would be ready. His target would not be tree branches, frightened rabbits or broken bottles.

It would be time for vengeance and he had to be ready for that.

★ ★ ★

Carla stood at the top of the wide circular staircase that led from the bar room and looked over the rail at the only table that interested her. She had managed to shake off the unwanted attentions of a pawing, drink-fuelled cowhand and could now consider her next move.

She had thought long and hard about how she could get rid of Jay and at the same time get her hands on the money they had taken from Mitchell Dredge.

Downstairs, Munroe was engrossed in the card game — the actions of Carla would be the last thing on his mind as he eyed the pile of notes and coins in the middle of the table.

Turning, she made her way to the room she sometimes shared with him. She had scribbled a short message exposing her lover she knew would trigger McCabe's curiosity, but he might ignore such a note, dismissing it as an attempt to poison the name of an innocent party, especially if the note was left unsigned as Carla had intended. But if she went to see him in person, maybe that would convince him.

She had asked around town about McCabe and discovered that he lived at Widow Fraser's boarding-house and, although considered to be a peace-loving, honest citizen, and an ex-lawman, he had a reputation as a man who stood against injustice. Just the man to go after Munroe.

Checking again that Jay was still deep into his card game, Carla slipped out of the saloon and headed for the widow's house at the end of the street. With any luck she would find Ben McCabe at home . . .

That still left her with the problem of

how to get her hands on the money, but a plan was forming in her mind.

Darkness had fallen over Charlsburg and the streets were deserted. The town's respectable citizens were in their homes, discussing the day's events, for what they were worth, and the only lights came from the three saloons, the newspaper building and the sheriff's office. But Carla needed no guiding lights to lead her to the boarding-house on the outskirts of town.

The gate of the picket fence surrounding the neatly kept two-storey building was open and there was a dim light behind the lace curtains in the front window. Carla knocked and waited, convincing herself she had made the right decision. She wanted Jay dead and she believed that, when Ben McCabe knew what she had to say, he was the man to kill him.

Eventually her knock was answered by a woman she recognized as the owner of the boarding-house, the widow Agnes Fraser.

Agnes eyed her visitor with curiosity.

'I'm looking for Ben McCabe,' Carla said, without preamble. 'I've got something that might interest him.'

Agnes looked at her caller more closely. She was attractive in a vulgar way — not the sort of woman she imagined her favourite tenant would have on his list of female acquaintances. She was a year or two younger than Agnes herself and maybe a head taller. Unlike many of Charlsburg's women she was of pale complexion, as though she spent her days indoors.

'He's not here,' Agnes said curtly, her voice cold and unwelcoming. 'Can I help?'

Carla grinned. 'It's between me and . . . and Ben,' she said suggestively. 'Do you know where I can find him?'

'You could try the sheriff's office,' Agnes said evasively, 'or The Silver Lady.'

Agnes was reluctant to mention the saloon. She liked to believe that Ben wasn't like the rest of Charlsburg's male inhabitants who spent much of their time in the town's bars and gambling halls. Though she did know that, just like those others, he enjoyed the occasional drink and card game.

Carla already knew that McCabe was not in the saloon and the sheriff was the last person she wanted to hear what she had to say. She reached inside her shirt pocket and pulled out the note. She handed it to Agnes.

'Would you give him this? Tell him . . . ' She hesitated. 'Tell him — no, nothing. Just give him the note. He'll know what to do.'

She turned to leave but Agnes reached out and gripped her arm. 'Can I tell him who left this?'

Carla shook herself free. 'He doesn't need to know. It's not important. Just see that he gets the message.'

Agnes stood on her doorstep and watched the woman march off down the path and into the night. But hers were not the only pair of eyes watching as Carla closed the gate behind her and strode off towards the town.

* * *

The moon had disappeared behind the gathering rain clouds when Carla started back from the Fraser boarding-house to the saloon. She had been tempted to call in at the sheriff's office to seek out McCabe, but decided against it. She did not want to alert the law and risk losing the $20,000 or so that Jay had stacked away. Leaving McCabe to dispose of Munroe gave her the best chance of keeping the where-abouts of the money secret.

She hurried along the main street, eager to get back to the Silver Lady. If she was not there when Jay finally threw in his hand there would be trouble. She had to be where he wanted her to be when he wanted her.

She had come to hate the thought of Munroe touching her. At first he had been attentive and caring, a welcome change from her brutal and uncouth but now happily departed husband, Vic. But, over time, that had changed. The drinking, the gambling had taken hold. Jay had become sour and twisted although he had never resorted to the violence of Vic — until he put the second bullet in Mitchell Dredge. Carla had watched him enjoying the moment. It was enough to convince her that she could not stay with him: to do so would mean an early grave and that was not part of her plans.

The lack of moonlight and the absence of any street lamps did not worry Carla. She knew all the back alleys and, hurrying past the barber shop and general store, she left the main street and headed for the rear entrance of the saloon. That way, Jay would have no idea that she had left while he was preoccupied with his card game. She felt herself hoping he'd had a successful night. More losing hands would leave him in a foul temper and that in turn led to more drinking.

She was less than fifty yards from the outside staircase that she had used earlier when the figure stepped out of the shadows in front of her.

Startled, she stopped dead in her tracks.

'Holy God, Jay, you almost frightened the life out of me!'

He grinned, that same crooked grin that he wore so often but revealed so little.

'Wouldn't want to do that now, Carla, would I?' he smirked.

Did she imagine it or was there menace in his voice?

'Where've you been?'

It wasn't a question she had been prepared for. Did he know? How could he? He had been playing cards.

'I — er — I needed some air,' she said feebly, her voice barely more than a stammer. 'All that smoke in the saloon — it was getting to me.'

His grin broadened, became more twisted.

'That so?' he said, moving closer to her. 'After all this time the little lady's worried about a bit of cigar smoke. You shoulda waited for me to finish the game. My luck was in. We could have had a stroll together. You know how I like that. Walking out with a pretty woman on my arm.'

Was he teasing her? Toying with her? He ran his fingers down her cheek.

''Cept I can't quite believe you. I think you went out for more than a breath of air. Leastways that's how it looks.'

All she could offer was a nervous laugh. 'I don't know what you mean, Jay, here I am rushing back to be there for you when you finished the card game.'

'D'you know something, Carla, I wish I could believe that, I truly do. But you see, I have people looking out for me so when I was told that you had slipped out the back, I just wondered . . . '

'What, Jay? What are you saying?'

'Well, first I thought I'd take a look-see. Maybe she was seeing another feller and I wouldn't like that either.'

Only then did Carla realize what he was saying.

'So . . . you followed me?' she asked nervously. Carla felt her throat tighten. She was suddenly gripped by real fear. She wanted to turn, to run, but that would be useless. She had seen how Jay dealt with people who tried to get away from him. Like that railroad man, Mitchell Dredge. Was she next?

'You went to see your friend Ben McCabe,' he said quietly, the smile suddenly vanishing as his mood became black. 'Why did you do that, Carla?'

Although the night was warm, she shivered.

'No, Jay, I went to see the widow woman, Mrs Fraser. Like I said, the saloon is getting me down. I wondered if she had a room to spare. That's all.'

The grin returned.

'So, first you wanted some air, now you want to rent a room. Why am I not believing any of this? You know what I think? I think you went along to sell me out.' His voice rose, his ice-cold eyes were staring and full of hatred.

'No, Jay, no — you know that's not — '

The protest died with her. As Jay pulled her towards him she expected to feel his arms wrap around her and his lips press on hers. She did not see his right hand move to his back, withdraw the knife from its sheath and plunge it deep into her stomach.

She gasped her last as she slumped to the ground, blood oozing from the fatal wound.

★ ★ ★

Sheriff Brad Nicholls nodded occasionally, adding his comments and suggestions only when he was asked. His visitor, Ben McCabe, sat opposite him across the side desk. He was deep in thought.

The two men had spent a full hour discussing the killing of Mitchell Dredge and the disappearance of the money from the rail-company's safe.

'Whoever killed him will be well out of the territory by now,' Nicholls suggested, 'and twenty thousand dollars richer.'

But McCabe was not convinced. 'Maybe not, Sheriff.' He rose from his chair and strode across the room to stare out into the night. 'Whoever shot Dredge didn't kill him because of the cut of his suit. The killer knew all about the money he was carrying.'

'So you reckon it was somebody Dredge knew?'

McCabe rubbed his chin. 'More than that. At least, I think so. I'm pretty sure we've been missing something. Remember, Dredge robbed the company at least twice. The first time I happened to be out of town on my way to see my sister. He used that to point the finger at me — even sent out Wanted posters all around the county with a price on my head. Then he ran out after emptying the safe during that ruckus with the cattlemen when he tried to put up their charges. That was nothing to do with the company — just another Dredge scheme to make fast bucks. I knew Dredge — he couldn't have done any of that without help.'

'So you're saying that somebody here in Charlsburg was in on the whole robbery and the murder?'

'That's just what I'm saying, Sheriff. And, besides, this is personal. Somebody shot me and left me for dead in that creek. If it hadn't been for those two young brothers and their grandpa, the job would have been done. He may even have thought he'd finished me and collected the reward. Then that crooked lawman Miller and his young sidekick came gunning for me — '

'But you said you shot Miller and scared off the kid,' Nicholls interrupted.

'Sure, I got Miller, but I don't know how bad. Far as I know there's three guns out there who want to finish me off. Like I said, it's personal.' The two men fell silent for a moment before the sheriff said, 'If you're right then the man who gunned you down is likely to be the same one who killed Dredge.'

'Thieves falling out?' Ben asked.

'Makes sense I suppose. Trouble is, Brad, we don't know who we're looking for. It could be anybody, and he might already know that I'm walking around looking for him.'

Nicholls nodded. 'He'll also know that you don't know who he is. That gives him the edge, don't you think? He can pick his time to finish the job he started.'

Ben chuckled. 'Thanks for that cheery news. Looks like I have to find him before he gets me. And — '

He was interrupted by a loud banging on the door and a man dressed in a barman's apron burst into the room. Nicholls spun round.

'What's wrong, Charlie? You look like you seen a ghost!'

'Worse than that, Sheriff,' gasped the man called Charlie, desperately trying to get his breath. 'There's been a killing. You gotta come.'

Nicholls picked his hat off the peg and buckled on his gunbelt. 'Lead the way, Charlie. Who's been killed?'

Charlie struggled with his emotions. 'It ain't pretty, Sheriff. It's one of the girls from the saloon. She's been knifed. It's Carla Blake.'

14

Ben spent a restless night in his room at the back of Agnes Fraser's boarding-house. Across the passage, he could hear his sister sobbing, then talking in her sleep, crying out in imagined pain.

Tomorrow, Agnes would accompany Emily on the train journey to Chicago where she would go into a special hospital for women suffering from mental disorders brought on by ordeals inflicted on them by brutes such as Tobias Troon.

McCabe took comfort in the knowledge that his troubled sister would be in good hands once she reached Chicago and he was grateful to Agnes for accompanying her on the journey. Meanwhile there was the message that had been waiting for him on his return to the house. He had left the sheriff's office when the lawman was called out to the murder of a saloon girl in the alley behind the Silver Lady.

The message was short, written in a neat, woman's hand on good quality notepaper.

If you want to know who killed the railroad man talk to Jay Munroe.

No name. No signature. And Agnes did not know the woman who had delivered the note.

Maybe this was the break McCabe needed. He had thought the trail had gone cold but now . . . tomorrow he would seek out Mr Munroe.

* * *

The trance-like state of his sister worried Ben when he saw the two women off on the East-bound train. His own problems seemed so insignificant and he wondered whether he should be the one accompanying the disturbed Emily on her journey, but, as the train disappeared around the bend, he tried to shake off the growing feeling that he would never see his sister again. She was nothing more than a shell of the vital, fun-loving young girl she had been before Tobias Troon entered her life.

He turned away from the rail depot and headed for the sheriff's office. He hoped Brad Nicholls would be at his desk. He needed to know more about Jay Munroe before he challenged the man named in the note that had been waiting for him.

He was in luck. Nicholls was in his office, but he looked tired, as though he hadn't slept throughout the night. He clearly hadn't shaved, and the grey-speckled bristle added to the drained appearance.

He tried a cheery 'Morning, Ben', but McCabe knew he was in anything but good humour. He was slumped in his chair behind the desk clearly deep in thought.

'Nobody heard anything; nobody saw

anything. It's as though the poor woman was knifed to death by a ghost,' he said in frustration.

'It's usually the way,' McCabe offered.

'Maybe the killer was waiting for her. Knew where she would be and when.'

The sheriff nodded. 'But why? She was a saloon singer, liked by most of the men who use the Silver Lady. Nobody thought bad of her.'

'Somebody did,' McCabe said. 'The killer. I wish you luck, Sheriff, but I doubt whether you'll ever find who did this. A pretty saloon girl — I suppose she was pretty? — can stir up a few hot bloods.'

Nicholls thought for a moment. 'You think this was a jealousy killing? Could be. Carla had a lot of admirers.'

'Then you'll need that luck.'

'All part of the job of being sheriff. But what brings you out this early? I thought your sister was off to Chicago for treatment.'

'The train left fifteen minutes ago. Mrs Fraser's gone with her, left me looking after the boarding-house for the next few days.'

Nicholls chuckled. 'And I thought I had a tough job.'

McCabe pulled the note out of his shirt pocket. 'I had a visitor last night. She left this.'

He handed over the note which Nicholls scoured before asking, 'Who left it?'

'Didn't leave a name. Agnes said she didn't know her. Why?'

Nicholls handed the note back.

'Jay Munroe. When I said our dead woman had a long list of admirers — you could put that name on that list. And Dredge's.'

The two men exchanged glances as though they were both thinking along the same lines.

It was McCabe who spoke.

'You reckon it might have been the dead woman who delivered this message?'

The sheriff didn't answer. Ben McCabe folded the note, replaced it in his shirt pocket and left the office.

What did Jay Munroe know about the killing of Mitchell Dredge? Was he the killer? And if he was, had he knifed Carla Blake to death after she left the Fraser house? Was he trying to silence her?

McCabe knew that he would have to tread carefully. From what he was piecing together Jay Munroe sounded like a dangerous man.

Leaving the sheriff's office, he made his way back to the railroad office. There were things to do before he challenged Munroe with the note . . .

★　★　★

Little more than a day's ride away, the young gunman used the remains of his half-finished coffee to kill off the fading embers of his camp-fire. He threw his saddle over the grazing chestnut and gathered his bedroll. He was ready to face the man he had sworn to kill.

★　★　★

The murder of Carla Blake was a talking point among the patrons of the Silver Lady but it did nothing to dampen their zest for a night of music and gambling. The saloon was buzzing with activity when McCabe entered the smoke-filled bar late that evening.

He had spent the day in the railroad office, searching through desks and boxes in an attempt to find any link between Dredge, Munroe and the murdered woman. If there was one, the deceased depot manager had kept it well hidden. McCabe had left empty-handed.

The man who had come rushing into the sheriff's office to report the stabbing was behind the bar, polishing glasses and refilling those emptied by a group of cowhands standing near the piano. Across the room card players sat silently studying their hands while a singer weaved her way between the tables.

McCabe ordered a beer and studied the wide range of customers from impressionable young cowboys to hard-headed old-timers. Somewhere among them he suspected was a man called Jay Munroe.

'He'll be around,' the barman confirmed. 'Comes in every night for a few hands . . . and maybe a woman later,' he added, offering a look that said he didn't miss much of what happened in the Silver Lady.

McCabe sipped his beer. He had time to wait for Munroe to put in an appearance. He was halfway through his second drink when Charlie the barman edged towards him.

'That's Munroe,' he said, pointing towards the balcony.

A tall, slim, black-shirted man was staggering along the passage with a woman clinging to his arm. They were laughing like a pair of young lovers and, when the woman pulled him towards her, he submitted easily and the two went into a clinch. Then, suddenly releasing her, Munroe pushed her to one side, leaned over the handrail and signalled towards one of the card tables. He was clearly ready for his night of gambling and if Carla Blake had meant anything to him she belonged in the past: her death was a trifling episode in his life.

McCabe gulped the last of his beer, slid the empty jug along the bar and headed for the staircase. He met Munroe at the foot of the stairs.

He was thin-faced, pale-complexioned with a twisted mouth that appeared to be locked in a permanent grin. His blue eyes drilled deep into McCabe as he stood and blocked the way into the bar room. There was a brief face-to-face silence before Ben spoke.

'I'm told you're Jay Munroe.'

The other man frowned, though strangely the grin never left his face. He said nothing.

'My name's Ben McCabe. I need to talk.'

Munroe visibly relaxed. 'Sorry, Mr Ben McCabe, I'm busy. Maybe some other time.'

He moved to go but Ben stood in his path.

'Now that's not very friendly. Not when I've been waiting for you to ask for your help.' He tried to sound relaxed but made sure that he got his message across. 'Let me buy you a drink.'

Munroe shrugged his thin shoulders and reluctantly followed Ben to the bar. The barman did not need to be told before pouring Ben another beer and a long shot of whiskey for Munroe.

'Let's take a seat. It's more private,' Ben suggested, and without waiting led the way to an empty table. The two men sat opposite each other and, as Ben raised his glass he said, 'You look uneasy, Munroe. Anything wrong?'

Munroe shrugged again. 'Who are you and what do you want? Like I said, I'm busy.'

McCabe produced the note from his shirt and slid it across the table. Munroe unfolded it slowly, read the message and then pushed the piece of paper back across the table. He said nothing.

McCabe stared at him over the rim of his beer glass.

'Somebody thinks you know who killed Mitchell Dredge,' he said, after a long silence.

Munroe toyed with his glass. He didn't look McCabe in the eye.

'Sorry, mister. Don't think I know anybody called Dredge. Who is he?'

'Was.' McCabe's voice was sharp. 'Like the note said — he's dead. He worked for the railroad, but I reckon you knew that much.'

Munroe emptied his glass and rose to leave, but Ben grabbed his wrist. 'Sit down!' he ordered. 'I haven't finished.'

But Munroe's confidence was growing. When he ran into McCabe at the foot of the stairs his first thoughts were that the railroad agent had discovered who had put two bullets in him and left him for dead by that creek. That he was there to get even.

But now it was obvious that the man

knew nothing. He was shooting in the dark.

'Listen, McCabe, you come in here with this' — he waved angrily at the note on the table — 'and expect me to know who killed somebody I've never even met.' His voice was rising in anger, his self assurance fully restored. 'Who gave you this?'

'A woman left it for me last night.'

'A woman! What woman?'

'I thought you might tell me. Carla Blake, maybe? She was murdered last night. Don't tell me you didn't know her?'

Munroe sat back in his chair. He raised the whiskey glass to his lips before remembering that it was empty.

'Sure, I knew Carla. Every man in Charlsburg knew her.' He paused, then added, 'She was a special woman.'

'Is that what got her killed?' Ben leaned forward and waved the notepaper in front of Munroe's face. 'Or was it this? Did she know too much?'

This time Munroe held his stare.

'Listen, McCabe, you don't even know if it was Carla who left that message. It could have been anybody, somebody with a grudge against me. There are a few women I have had in my life . . . and, like I said, I don't know anything about this man Dredge. I — ' He suddenly fell silent. He was letting his anger get the better of him. The note had not said that he had killed Dredge, only that he knew something about it. 'I can't help you. Like I said, I'm busy.'

McCabe watched him walk purposefully across the room and take his place at one of the card tables. He nodded at the other players, withdrew a pile of notes from his pocket and called for the man holding the cards to deal. McCabe studied him for some time. He had learned nothing from the meeting other than the feeling that Munroe was a cold-hearted devil.

He also knew that Munroe was no innocent caught up in something he knew nothing about but there was nothing he could prove. He did not know if Carla had been the woman who delivered the note, but nor did he believe in coincidence. With Agnes now on her way to Chicago he couldn't even call on her to look at the dead woman.

He was certain that the killing and the note were linked . . . and somewhere in there was Jay Munroe.

Ben finished his beer and rose from the table. He walked across to the bar and called over the bartender but shook his head when he was offered another beer.

'The woman who was killed last night — Carla — she had a room here?'

'Top of the stairs at the end of the passage,' said Charlie. 'Why?'

McCabe did not offer an answer. Instead he bounded up the stairs, along the corridor to the rooms at the back of the saloon.

The door to Carla Blake's room was unlocked. Inside it was much as he had expected — an iron bedstead, a dressing-table and padded stool, a closet full of a saloon-singer's working costumes of frills and a bedside table complete with jug and bowl. There was also a small writing bureau in the far corner.

Without knowing what he was looking for McCabe searched through the closet, then the drawers. And finally the desk. It was there that he found what he was hoping to see. Taking the note from his shirt, he compared it with the sheets of notepaper piled neatly in the top drawer of the bureau.

They were identical. Carla *had* written the message — and Jay Munroe was implicated. It was time to challenge him again.

★　★　★

Down in the bar room, Munroe had watched McCabe climb the staircase. He threw in his cards and rose from the table. Without a word he scooped up the pile of notes and coins in front of him and headed for the bar. Charlie saw him coming and moved away, eager to pretend he was busy doing a barman's chores. He didn't like Jay Munroe. Nobody liked him, but Charlie had more reason than most to hate his guts.

Jay had been nothing more than an unruly kid when he had lied to implicate Charlie in a theft from the general store where they both worked. The store was owned by Jay's stepfather, but he had given Charlie the job of running it. He had been told to keep an eye on young Jay who had already shown signs of taking the wrong path. It soon became obvious that young Munroe was going to be a handful and when he took to pilfering Charlie knew that it was time to act. Jay had been working at the store as a messenger boy delivering supplies to customers living on the outskirts of Charlsburg and the smaller settlements beyond. But when Charlie discovered that Jay was taking out more than he was delivering he challenged him only to learn that the young rebel had been supplying farmers with the extras he was carrying. Jay had bluffed his way out by accusing Charlie and when the old man discovered discrepancies in the bookkeeping and cash missing he made the mistake of siding with his lying stepson.

In addition Jay had planted stolen property in Charlie's barn and that clinched it for the old man. For some time nobody would employ Charlie. Being sacked by the town's leading citizen was hardly a recommendation to other businessmen to take him on, however much they needed the help.

Eventually he found work as a hotel clerk and barman but his standing in Charlsburg had plummeted. The citizens of the expanding Wyoming settlement knew young Jay for what he was, but his stepfather was a popular mayor and when he spoke up for the boy, effectively condemning Charlie, they listened. Charlie became the outcast and Jay gloated.

Reluctantly, he threw down his bar towel and walked over to where

Munroe was standing.

'What did you tell him?'

Charlie played dumb.

'Who?'

Munroe leaned across and reached for Charlie's shirt front.

'Don't mess with me. You know what happens when you do. McCabe — what did you tell him?'

Charlie suddenly realized he felt no fear. He slowly removed Jay's hand from his shirt. He even managed to smile.

'I told him what he wanted to know — why don't you ask him?'

'Listen, I ruined you once and I'll do it again.'

'Not any more, Jay. You've done your worst. McCabe's going to find out all about you and, when he does, he'll finish you.'

He turned away and left the seething Munroe standing alone at the bar. He stayed there for a moment undecided what to do next.

He had killed Carla to silence her, but had he been too late? She had given his name to McCabe and the man was no fool. How much did he already know? Why had he gone rushing up the stairs? One secret was still safe. McCabe could not know that Munroe was the man who had left him for dead and collected the reward that Dredge had put on his head.

Maybe the time had come to move on. He had lived in Charlsburg for all his twenty-three years. There were other towns out there where he could make a new start. What was left of the $20,000 he had taken from Dredge would keep him going.

Abruptly he turned away from the bar. There was no time like now. McCabe was still upstairs searching Carla's room. It was time to get out of town.

★ ★ ★

Brad Nicholls took pride in his job. He was a good lawman. Honest to the point that the law was everything to him. He had always done his best to honour the badge that he wore on on his shirt.

But as he sat and listened to Ben McCabe's story he wondered how much longer he could hold on to that claim. Slowly he pushed the two pieces of notepaper to one side, got to his feet and walked across the room.

McCabe had made his way from the saloon to the sheriff's office. He had told Nicholls of his run-in with Jay Munroe, of his search of Carla's room and his discovery of the notepaper now lying on the office desk. 'Munroe killed Dredge,' Ben said confidently. 'I'm sure of it.'

The sheriff turned to face his visitor. He had come to like Ben McCabe. He had even given him a deputy's star so that he could go in search of the runaway Dredge with at least a pretence of legal authority. But the look on his face was not of admiration or affection when he eventually spoke.

'Look, Ben, this could all be chance. Two pieces of notepaper are not proof

— only that it looks as though Carla wrote the note. We can't pull in Jay on that evidence.'

Ben McCabe studied the sheriff closely. What was wrong? Why was he so reluctant to believe that Munroe had killed Dredge and then knifed Carla to silence her? He felt his anger rising and he spoke louder than he intended.

'What's wrong, Sheriff? Munroe's got to be the man we're looking for. I told you, he even — '

'Acted guilty,' Nicholls interrupted hurriedly. 'Hell, I can't arrest a man for acting like he's guilty.'

Ben picked up the two sheets of Carla's notepaper and after studying them again he said, 'There's more than that, though. Tell me, Brad, what is it about Munroe? What's he got on you?'

It was a shot in the dark but it hit the target.

'I can't bring Jay in, Ben. He's family.'

McCabe gasped — he hadn't expected this.

'Family?'

Nicholls slumped into his chair. To McCabe, he looked like a man who had reached the moment he had dreaded but knew would arrive some day. 'Jay Munroe isn't only the mayor's stepson, he's my wife's brother.'

The two men fell silent. Ben McCabe was convinced that Munroe was the man he wanted, but he knew he could hardly call on the local sheriff to turn in his wife's own kin. If Jay Munroe was ever going to face justice it would be at McCabe's hands.

15

The Silver Lady was in semi-darkness when McCabe returned after his meeting with the sheriff. Old Charlie was sweeping the floor and a drunk whom McCabe recognized as the piano player was slumped across a table at the far end of the room. There was no sign of Munroe.

Charlie stopped sweeping and leaned on his broom.

'You lookin' for our friend Jay?'

McCabe nodded.

'He's gone.'

'I can see that, old man. Gone where?'

'Didn't say. Just went upstairs, collected his gear and was out of here faster than a polecat with its tail on fire. Something you said musta really got him. I ain't never seen Jay so scared in all my days.'

McCabe thought about that. So

Munroe was on the run. A sign that he was the guilty man? He was about to pump Charlie for more information about Munroe's likely escape route when the two men were interrupted by the appearance of a woman at the saloon doors. She was dressed in a black, hooded cloak and she stopped on the threshhold. nervous, hesitant, unsure of her next few steps. It was Charlie who moved across to meet her.

'Can I help you, miss? You look kinda lost.'

The woman removed her hood to reveal a head of long flowing fair hair crowning a pretty young face. When she spoke her voice was barely above a timid whisper.

'I'm looking for a Mr McCabe. The sheriff said I might find him here.'

'You've found him,' McCabe said, moving towards the visitor. As he got close he realized she was little more than a girl, barely twenty years of age. The eyes of her pretty elfin face had been reddened by much crying. She was clearly a distressed young lady.

McCabe took her arm and led her to a nearby table. He waved towards Charlie.

'Bring the young lady a drink, Charlie, and not that rotgut whiskey you pour down the throats of your regular customers.'

He eased the girl into a seat and waited for her to speak. For a time she stayed silent, dabbing her eyes with a silk handkerchief. She sat like a frightened child but finally muttered, almost inaudibly, 'She wasn't a bad person, Mr McCabe. Not all bad.'

'Who?'

'My sister,' the girl stammered, her voice still little more than a whisper. 'Carla is — was — my sister.' The revelation started the girl sobbing again. 'She didn't deserve to die like that. Whatever she had done.'

McCabe reached across the table and took the girl's hand.

'Why don't you tell me about it, Miss — ?'

'Jennifer. Carla was a few years older than me.' She stopped sobbing and McCabe sat and listened with as much patience as he could muster as she falteringly told him why she had searched for him.

She began nervously. 'Our father was a brutal man, Mr McCabe. He regularly beat my mother in his state of drunkenness. Carla and I were spared the same punishment only because our brother stood up to him. James took a few beatings on our behalf. Our father was eventually shot to death on his way home from the saloon one night. Nobody was ever arrested for the killing but Carla and I knew who did it.

'We never spoke about it and our brother never said anything, but we knew — we knew he had gone out that night and killed the man we all hated.

'By then Carla had left home. She thought she had escaped, but the man she married was just another version of our father — a drunken, wife-beating brute. Luckily for Carla he suffered the

229

same fate — though this time Danny had nothing to do with it. There were countless volunteers who would have cheerfully put a bullet in Vic Blake.

'Carla never trusted any man again — she used them to get what she wanted. She is — she was — very attractive to men. Perhaps not beautiful but . . . exciting.'

She hesitated, taking another sip of the drink Charlie had brought her. While she was silent, McCabe was starting to wonder where all this was leading.

'Why are you telling me this, Jennifer?' he asked.

'My sister used men, Mr McCabe. She took delight in pitting them against each other. She had long ago abandoned any morals. I tried to get her to go back to the way we were, but she just laughed at me. The way we were for Carla was life with a vicious father and then a violent husband. She wanted none of that — even though both men are now

230

dead. She said I was being young and foolish and one day I would see men for what they really are — animals, she said, worse than coyotes.'

'Men like Mitchell Dredge? And Jay Munroe?'

The girl nodded.

'Just like them,' she sighed. She took another drink. 'Two nights ago I overheard Carla and Munroe arguing violently. I was calling on her to come and visit . . . Mother's quite ill and I thought Carla would like to see her before . . . before she dies.

'I came in up the back stairs. I don't like coming to places like this, Mr McCabe, and I had just reached Carla's room when I heard their raised voices. I stopped at the door and I listened.'

McCabe waited. The silence suggested that the young woman did not know how to continue.

'They were arguing about the money they had taken from Mitchell Dredge after Munroe had killed him. Jay was trying to involve Carla in the killing

— she had been Dredge's, er, mistress' — the word seemed to horrify her — 'at the same time that she was seeing Munroe. As I said she liked to play one man against another.'

McCabe raised his hand to silence her.

'You're sure? This is what you heard — that Jay Munroe killed Dredge?'

The girl nodded. 'But that's not everything I heard, Mr McCabe.'

Ben waited. He could see that the girl was distressed and wondering whether she should continue.

Tightly gripping her handkerchief, she forced herself to finish her story.

'He told her that Dredge had been lying — that he had collected only two thousand dollars not five thousand — for killing a man he now knew was still alive. Then he said the name. I heard it very clearly, Mr McCabe. Jay Munroe said that Mr Dredge and the rail company had paid him the money as a reward for killing you.'

16

In the days that followed, Ben McCabe rode in search of the man who had left him for dead; the man who had killed Mitchell Dredge and robbed him of $20,000 belonging to the rail company; and in all likelihood, had plunged the knife into the stomach of Carla Blake.

As soon as he had escorted young Jennifer safely to her home, he had returned to the sheriff's office to find Brad Nicholls locking up for the night. They had stood on the dimly lit boardwalk while McCabe retold the story that had been related to him less than an hour before.

'I can understand why you can't bring him in, Brad, with your family loyalties. Besides, he will be well outside your jurisdiction now, but I'm going after him and, if I can I'm going to bring him back alive. To face trial. The rest will be up to you.'

Nicholls rested a hand on his new friend's shoulder. 'If Jay's the killer he'll get what's coming to him, family or not. You have my word on it. You've still got that star I gave you when you went after Dredge — it won't fool Jay, but — well, it's the best I can do.'

The two men shook hands. 'That's good enough for me,' McCabe said.

That night he returned to the Fraser house and scribbled a note for Agnes. She was due to return from Chicago the following day, having left Emily at the hospital. He promised to return within the week. If he had not tracked down Jay Munroe by then he would give up the chase and curse the fact that the man who had been paid to kill him would go free.

One week. To kill — or be killed? Only time would tell.

After a short, restless sleep, McCabe loaded up with provisions, mounted his horse and, as dawn broke over the eastern ridge, set out on his mission.

A string of small towns, isolated farmhouses and deserted cabins brought no hints of the whereabouts of Munroe and McCabe was on the fourth day of his quest when he got the first news that he was on the right trail.

He had planned to stay over at the little out of the way town of Rockford, restock his supplies and spend the night in a comfortable hotel room as a change from the camp-fire and a bedroll under the stars.

The Rockford Hotel stood across the street from the small saloon and, after securing his room at the hotel, McCabe made his way over to enjoy a quiet drink — his first since leaving Charlsburg.

The bar was a cheerless dim room with only a handful of customers engaged in private conversation. And they fell totally silent when McCabe pushed open the creaking batwing doors and headed for the bar. Strangers were not common in Rockford.

The bartender was a thickset man

who clearly had the physique and the know-how to control unruly clientele — it would have taken an excessive state of drunkenness to challenge such an imposing figure.

He greeted McCabe with a questioning glare that didn't offer any welcoming warmth.

'What can I get you?' he asked peevishly.

McCabe tried a smile, but it cut no ice with the barman.

'I'll have a beer.'

He looked round at the empty tables, silent piano and deserted stage.

'Quiet in here tonight,' he said, as the barman slid the jug of beer across the counter in his direction.

'It's how we like it, mister,' he said. 'Quiet.' Then he walked away ending any chance McCabe had of drawing him into useful conversation.

'But it ain't allus so.'

The speaker, a wiry, grey-bearded man nursing half a jug of ale, edged along from the far end of the bar to where McCabe was standing. 'Hank likes to think he keeps an orderly house, but you shoulda been here last night. Sure was some excitement.'

McCabe smiled. The town busybody was ready to take centre stage and, despite a warning look from the barman, he wasn't going to be silenced. Giving the stranger the lowdown on the previous night's activities would, he guessed, earn him at least another beer.

'We don't see too many strangers around here, mister, so you ain't too welcome by some folk. Now me, I'll have a drink with you if you're buying.'

McCabe quickly formed the opinion that the man would drink with anybody who was buying, but he let it pass. He needed information and if the only source was the local gossip merchant then so be it.

He called the barman over and ordered a refill for his new companion.

The man grinned, exposing a row of tobacco-stained and broken teeth.

'Like you mighta guessed, mister, we

don't take too kindly to strangers in Rockford and last night we had our fill of 'em so you'll have to forgive us if we don't make you feel too welcome.'

Ben ignored the implied taunt. 'What happened last night?'

The man slurped his beer and tried to chuckle at the same time.

'We had our first ruckus in years and it was all over a cheating stranger.'

The man related the story of a card game that ended with a bloody brawl that spilled out over on the sidewalk and ended with the stranger being run out of town.

'He was lucky there was no tar and feathers handy or he'd'a got it for sure.' The man cackled again and this time McCabe joined him. He needed more from the man.

'What did he look like — this stranger?'

'Aw, scrawny sort, long hair, but fancied himself with the women from what I could see.'

'Where was he from?'

'Huh? He didn't say, but I sure as hell know which way he was going. My guess is that he wouldn't stop until his horse dropped dead under him, or he was safe the other side of Laramie.'

He emptied his beer glass with a flourish and ordered another which he expected McCabe to pay for.

'Tell you something else, too, mister: he was grinning all over his face when he got here, but we sure as hell wiped that crooked smile off his face before he left.'

★ ★ ★

Jay Munroe had fully recovered from his ordeal at the hands of the men he had cheated in that dump two nights earlier. Laramie was a much friendlier place; the women especially.

Munroe could still feel the effects of the kicking he had received outside that saloon but Lucy — that's what she said her name was — knew how to comfort him. Sure, it had cost him a few more bucks than he usually paid but she was worth it. There was only one other woman who even came close to giving him satisfaction, but even she had double-crossed him in the end. He had had to kill her and move on. Carla was in the past; there would be more like Lucy to fill his nights.

But now that he had paid her off it was time to get down to business. He was not in Laramie for its scenery of brickyard, slaughterhouse and brewery. This would be his last stop in Wyoming before he headed west to Nevada or maybe on to California. In the meantime there were suckers ready to be parted from their money at the card tables.

Dressed in a newly bought silver shirt, Munroe checked his appearance in the hotel-room mirror. Even if his luck with the cards deserted him there were sure to be other compensations. He buckled on his gunbelt, checked his billfold and headed down the stairs to the hotel's saloon.

An hour later he was well into a winning streak when Ben McCabe pushed open the doors and entered the room.

Munroe had intentionally chosen a table well away from the doors from where he could see who came in. He reckoned those louts from Rockford had long since given up chasing him, but it did no harm to be careful. It only needed a couple of them to go back and get themselves fuelled up with whiskey to boost their courage and come after him.

But the man who pushed open the batwings and stood scouring the room was no whiskey-charged small-town hick. And there was no doubting why he was in town.

Munroe killed the last of his drink, pulled the rim of his hat low over his eyes, scooped up his money and edged his way towards the back of the room. Initially, luck was on his side.

McCabe stood with his back to the bar and gazed around searchingly but there was enough saloon activity to hide Munroe as he moved to make his escape via the rear exit.

But the fates quickly turned against him.

'Hey, mister! You ain't walking out, not till we've had a chance to win back our money. Sit down!' The order was backed by a Colt that suddenly appeared in the man's left hand.

The other players got to their feet and Munroe found himself hemmed in a corner. He hadn't planned for this. What next? He glanced across the room — McCabe still hadn't made a move.

There was a tense stand-off before the man with the gun suddenly repeated his order. 'Sit down and deal the cards, mister.'

The man waved his gun and Jay knew he had no choice, until . . .

A sudden commotion broke out across the room when two worse-for-drink gamblers decided to compete for the attention of one of the dancers.

Jay seized his chance. Tipping over

the table, he leapt to his feet and rushed towards the back of the room. But the commotion was enough to alert McCabe. Munroe pushed his way past a bewildered old-timer but he found his way barred by a group of young cowboys in town on a celebration night. Munroe tried to fight his way past but there was no way through the crowd.

Before he knew what was happening he was bundled aside and he stumbled over a chair, crashing to the floor. All around the mixture of raucous laughter, shouts and curses grew louder as the confusion spilled over to other tables.

Scrambling to his feet, Munroe found himself looking into the face of the man who had hunted him down.

Instinctively, he reached for his gun, but McCabe was too quick for him. Lashing out with his boot, he aimed a vicious kick at Munroe and sent the gun spinning from his grasp. Jay screamed in pain.

'You've done enough killing!' McCabe snapped.

'You busted my arm, you bastard!'

McCabe leaned forward and dragged Munroe to his feet. Their faces were almost touching as he spat out his threat, 'You won't be needing it when I've finished. You'll be at the end of a rope.'

Around them the pandemonium grew as more drinkers joined the scattered fighting, but McCabe ignored them. He had got his man and he wasn't about to let him go. But Munroe, his injured arm throbbing, wasn't prepared to go along meekly. Ignoring the gun pointing at him, he swung his left arm and caught Ben high on the temple.

The blow did no damage but caught McCabe by surprise and boosted Munroe's sagging courage. Together the pair tumbled down two steps and on to the floor of the saloon. As they struggled to their feet the mayhem around them suddenly stopped. Men who had been throwing punches at each other stepped back to watch the two strangers act out their own private war.

The pair rolled across the floor before McCabe managed to free himself from Munroe's desperate clutches. He threw a wild punch, the pain jarring up his arm as he caught the other man flush on the jaw.

Another punch drew blood from Munroe's nose as the two were urged on by the gathering crowd of spectators. They struggled to their feet, but Munroe was sent reeling under the weight of another blow.

He was prevented from falling backwards when two of the young cowboys, eager to keep the fight alive, pushed him back into the fray. Trying to ignore the pain of his injuries, Munroe launched himself at McCabe, wrapping his arms around the bigger man so that they again ended up in a heap on the floor. This time McCabe quickly got the upper hand and Munroe was sent staggering by a flurry of punches.

Still he refused to give in and the

battle continued for several minutes before McCabe finally landed the blow that sent Jay into unconsciousness.

Brushing himself down and now watched by a fascinated but silent crowd, Ben McCabe dragged the groaning Munroe to his feet, replaced his hat and led him from the saloon.

A night in the cells followed by a train journey back to Charlsburg and Ben's job would be over. The rest would be up to Brad Nicholls and a judge.

★ ★ ★

Cy Cutler slammed the cell door and took another long look at the man behind the bars. He was in a sorry state, his face a mess of blood and bruises, his arm hanging limply at his side. He groaned loudly every time he moved.

'Looks like your man needs to see a doc,' said Cutler, returning to his office, where Ben was busy tending to his own bruises.

'He can see all the doctors he needs when I get him back to Charlsburg,' he answered sourly. 'I'm not inclined to worry about the health of somebody who put two bullets in me and left me for dead.'

The local marshal nodded. He settled into his chair and studied his visitor. The badge and the note from Brad Nicholls, Cutler's old army friend, had satisfied him that this man McCabe was on the right side of the law and needed his help.

'I reckon I'd feel the same if he did that to me. Want to talk about it?'

McCabe shrugged. He had gone over the events of the last few months many times in his mind but he had rarely talked about them. Maybe a sympathetic listener might help. 'It's a long story . . . '

Cutler listened without interruption while Ben told him how he came to track down Munroe.

He concluded, 'The man you've got locked away gunned me down when I was on my way to Ganson, a little town in Colorado, where my sister was locked in a sham of a marriage to the local preacher. I tracked him here to Laramie, and tomorrow he'll be back in Charlsburg to face trial. Even if Brad Nicholls is married to his sister,' he ended vehemently.

Cutler rose to his feet.

'Seems like you've had a hard time, McCabe. Glad I can be of help. The train leaves for Charlsburg at nine o'clock. I'll have your prisoner ready and waiting in plenty of time. Maybe you should get some sleep — he's going nowhere tonight.'

Ben thanked him but the job wasn't yet finished. There was still the matter of the money stolen first by Dredge and then by Munroe.

McCabe wanted it back, but, as he crossed the street and headed for Jay's hotel room to carry out his search, he wasn't sure that when he recovered the money he would return it to the company.

The battle with his conscience would occupy Ben for most of the night ahead.

★ ★ ★

McCabe knew he should have gained more satisfaction at the capture of Jay Munroe and he spent the train journey to Charlsburg wondering why he felt nothing. Munroe was a sneering, cold-hearted killer — two or three times over — and deserved to be dangling at the end of a rope but as he sat grim faced alongside McCabe, Ben had the uneasy feeling that the job was still not finished.

Despite his injuries, Munroe had remained cool and unconcerned when McCabe collected him from the jail-house in good time for the nine o'clock train to Charlsburg.

'This ain't over yet, McCabe. We ain't through, you and me,' he snarled through swollen lips. 'I should have finished you off down at the creek.'

'You had your chance, Jay, you won't get another.'

With Cy Cutler at the reins of the buggy the two fell silent for the rest of the short ride to the train depot.

Neither spoke again during the three-hour trip and when the locomotive pulled in to the small platform the sun was high in the Wyoming sky. The streets of Charlsburg were busy with midday shoppers and kids out of school eager to enjoy the spell of hot weather.

People stopped to stare at the two men — both bruised, but one with his arm in a makeshift sling, the other carrying a rifle and a gunbelt over his shoulder — making their way towards the sheriff's office.

Brad Nicholls was at his desk when McCabe pushed Jay into the room. It may have been his imagination, but McCabe was sure he saw the two men exchange glances before the lawman took Munroe into the cells at the rear of the building.

'I see you had a bit of trouble,' he

said, throwing the keys into his desk drawer. 'He's complaining about the way you smashed his arm and he wants me to arrest you.'

'Will you?' said Ben, removing the deputy star from his shirt and tossing it on to the desk.

'Guess not. I know Jay's through and through bad.'

'Thanks, Brad. He was a handful, but the badge and your letter made life easier even if he didn't come quietly. I think I'm about done here — it's time to move on.'

Nicholls picked up the discarded badge, examined it closely as though he had never seen it before.

'I reckon you'll have to stick around a time, Ben,' he said eventually. 'I told my wife Maggie — Jay's brother, like I told you — that you were going after him to bring him in, and she said she'd call in a top attorney from Cheyenne to defend him. Looks like we'll need you as a witness.'

McCabe nodded. He should have

known. After all, he was the only witness. Carla had paid for her part in the robbery with a knife in the stomach — a back-alley killing that nobody had seen. It was going to be McCabe's word against Jay's, and it was Munroe who had the smart lawyer.

So he had been right — it wasn't all over between them.

But all thoughts of a trial, attorneys and the law taking its course, were suddenly a problem for another day.

A single gunshot and shattering glass from the office window sent the two men diving for cover behind the desk.

'You in there, McCabe? Come on out — I'm calling you.'

The voice was rasping, almost a screech and it came from across the street. The two men exchanged glances before crawling out from behind the desk.

Cautiously Ben made his way to the smashed window and drew back the check curtains. A second gunshot was followed by another challenging shout.

'Are you coming out, McCabe — or am I coming in to get you?'

Keeping as low as he could, Ben peered out. The street, so busy and alive only a few minutes earlier, was now deserted. Except for one gunman standing in the shade cast by the Silver Lady Saloon. He was a slim figure in a white shirt, black vest and trousers and he was wearing a low-slung holster on his left hip.

'I'm waiting, McCabe, but I'm gettin' impatient! Are you yeller?'

Behind Ben, Brad Nicholls took his gunbelt from its wall hook and headed for the door. McCabe stepped in front of him.

'It's not your fight, Sheriff. I'm the one he wants.'

'This is my town, Ben, and we don't hold with street gunfights. Now step aside. I'm going out to talk to him.'

But McCabe refused to move. 'Listen, Brad, if it doesn't happen today, it'll happen tomorrow, or some other day. And it'll be here — in your town. This way it will be over.'

Nicholls hesitated. 'Who is he? Why does he want you?'

'That,' McCabe said, purposefully pushing past the lawman, 'is what I aim to find out.'

Without another word he stepped outside and into the sunlight.

It was the first time he had been able to get a good look at the man who had thrown out the challenge. He was little more than a kid — not yet twenty years of age if McCabe was any judge — and he was vaguely familiar. Where had they met before?

He wasn't given any time to think about that.

'I'm gonna kill you, McCabe. Just like you killed my partner.'

Puzzled, Ben decided it was time to stall.

'Your partner? I don't even know you or your . . . partner . . . ' His voice tailed off.

Suddenly it hit him. He *did* remember the kid who was calling him out.

Standing across the street ready to gun him down was the sidekick of the crooked lawman Ned Miller who had hunted him down to the Kane homestead. So . . . Miller had died from the gunshot wounds and this trigger-happy youth wanted his revenge.

The young man across the street sneered, 'Sure you remember me, McCabe. The name's Frank Beckman. I'm just telling you that so it's the last name you'll hear. I'm the one who's gonna put you in your grave. Now — draw, damn you!'

The talking was over. Ben was left with no choice and his Colt cleared leather in the blink of an eye.

But the kid was faster. In a flash, two shots shattered the still of the deserted street and two men fell face down in the sun-baked dust.

17

'You're a hard man to kill, Ben McCabe.'

Ben opened his eyes to gaze into the craggy features of Doc Riley. At his side, Agnes Fraser looked on anxiously.

'How's the kid?'

The doctor snorted. 'Like you — he'll live. But he won't be challenging anybody to a shoot-out for a long time. Your bullet smashed his left shoulder and when he fell he broke his wrist. Two injuries with one shot, you could say.'

Ben raised a smile. 'Good,' he said quietly. 'And what about me?'

Riley snorted again. 'One day, mister, you'll walk into a bullet and you won't walk away. But that's not my business. Right now, you're patched up and that's all I can do for you.'

'Thanks, Doc.'

He turned to Agnes. 'Thanks for taking Emily to Chicago — sorry I wasn't here when you got back.'

She smiled. 'Glad to help, but right now, I'm taking you back to the house. The doc here reckons you need a bit of nursing to get you back on your feet . . . '

A week later Ben McCabe scribbled another note for Agnes.

He was going to visit Emily in Chicago and then he would call on the Kane farm to assure the old man, the woman and her sons that he was not a killer on the run. He would leave the law to deal with Jay Munroe. Now that Frank Beckman had seen sense and decided to save his own hide by giving evidence against Munroe, even an expensive Cheyenne lawyer wouldn't be able to save Jay's neck.

McCabe finished the message by saying he hoped that one day he would be back in Charlsburg . . .

He left the note on the kitchen table while Agnes was in town shopping for the provisions she would eventually turn into a tasty meal for her guests.

Ben had thought long and hard about the money he had recovered.

He walked along to the stockyard, bought himself a fine-looking mare and rode out of Charlsburg for the last time with enough money in his saddle-bags to pay for Emily's treatment and give the Kanes enough to restock their farm. If the railroad company wanted their money back they would have to come looking for him.

THE END